||||| D0345911 |||||

This book is to be returned on or before the date above.
It may be borrowed for a further period if not in demand.

Essex County Council

GUANTANAMO
A NOVEL

by Dorothea Dieckmann

translated by Tim Mohr

DUCKWORTH OVERLOOK

First published in the UK in 2008 by
Duckworth Overlook
90-93 Cowcross Street, London EC1M 6BF
Tel: 020 7490 7300
Fax: 020 7490 0080
info@duckworth-publishers.co.uk
www.ducknet.co.uk

First published in the US in 2007 by
Soft Skull Press, New York

A catalogue record for this book is available
from the British Library

ISBN 978-0-7156-3600-8

Printed in Great Britain by
Creative Print & Design, Blaina, Wales

Honor Bound to Defend Freedom
—Slogan of the Joint Military Task Force
Guantanamo

Deeply lost in the night. Just as one sometimes lowers one's head to reflect, thus to be utterly lost in the night. All around people are asleep. It's just play acting, an innocent self-deception, that they sleep in houses, in safe beds, under a safe roof, stretched out or curled up on mattresses, in sheets, under blankets; in reality they have flocked together as they had once upon a time and again later in a deserted region, a camp in the open, a countless number of men, an army, a people, under a cold sky on cold earth, collapsed where once they had stood, forehead pressed on the arm, face to the ground, breathing quietly. And you are watching, are one of the watchmen, you find the next one by brandishing a burning stick from the brushwood pile beside you. Why are you watching? Someone must watch, it is said. Someone must be there.
—"At Night," by Franz Kafka, translated by
Tania and James Stern

Author's Note:

Guantanamo is an invention. It is one of the many inaccessible regions of the world. But I've been able to ground all the physical details here in fact: photographs and reports from journalists, the military, and from former prisoners held at the camp within the U.S. base in Cuba. (Only two scenes in chapter three use details from another U.S. base, at Bagram, near Kabul.) These sources are widely available to the public. As regards the inner details, only imagination can provide those, and the only imagination available to you is your own. The story I tell here is about imprisonment. In loosing my imagination on this topic, it was helpful to be tethered to reality.

Translator's Note

Italics in the original German text denote—as in English writing—foreign words and phrases. Many of these are in English. Here, of course, the English phrases would not otherwise be distinguished from the rest of the text. But we have opted to retain the italicization of all words—including English words—italicized in the original German manuscript.

1. *Down.* On your knees

This is where the journey ends. He has arrived. Somewhere on the face of the earth. That's all he knows. The light is gone and the noise has stopped, the droning, the vibrating, the lurching. Nothing is moving. They've left him alone. Time stands still. But it's not dark and it's not quiet. Everything that's happened is being compressed in his mind, everything's in flux. Even the pain doesn't stay in one spot, pulsing and flickering like the images and sounds. They swirl around. They can't escape. It's a closed system—they just chase each other around his head. Only one thing is fixed, a statement that keeps recurring over and over: *Don't move, don't worry, you are being taken home.*

There's the pain in his knees and the sound of his own breath in his ears. So he's alive. Not that he wants to know. But he can't shut his ears, can't close his eyes. He's already deaf, he's already blind—hears and sees only himself, without seeing beyond; he's locked in his own body, paralyzed. He looks for a way out, or a way back. He pokes at the space around him but finds himself pushing on parts of his own body. His head is shut, nothing can get in or out. Except the fog that sometimes fills it, impenetrable and numbing, as the images dissolve and he forgets how he got here, wrapped up, carried away, thrown out of the airplane, untied, chained up again, his hands in thick padded gloves, tape on his eyes and ears, hood over his head, his nose and mouth covered, thrown to the floor, left lying there, a heap of twisted flesh tangled up on itself.

Since he first knelt down to the ground, he has learned a lot. It starts with breathing. The openings end in a narrow chamber, a soft membrane in front of the nose and mouth. Air fills the mask. He pants slowly—mouth open, short flat breaths—until he gets dizzy, listening all the while to the sound of the breathing as if it weren't his own. Easy now, don't think, don't move. The floor is spinning. There's a rush in his skull. Hunched, bent over, he kneels in the heat and listens and dreams. The sound soothes him, washes over him, takes him away. This is how he'd like to remain, drifting on these waves, motionless, carried farther and farther away. Now the shallow current takes him even further—home, in the city, where it's cold and quiet. Everything is white and fluffy, but he knows the way. The snow absorbs the shallow, muffled footsteps and lost voices. Only car tires hiss loudly through the slush on the streets. He's arrived and everything is there, same as ever. The Jewish hospital is white as snow, and snow blankets the square behind it, the only dark spot a patch of rotting grass peeking out from under the gate. The fence is coated in ice. He sees himself turn onto Talstrasse, walk past the brick facades, down the sidewalk between the walls and little trees that line the street, and on towards the intersection. The white lines of the crosswalks are dirty and the bare stones of the building entranceways glisten with moisture. On the tiles beneath the awning of the cut-rate grocery store, bums huddle together. There's the bakery, Frau Roehlke waves from behind the shop window. A snow shovel leans against the front of the tattoo parlor, a couple of empty beer bottles sit on the steps next to the Lunacy Bar. Going home. Between the old buildings of Sielerstrasse the clouds hang low in the sky and the flag atop the kiosk is stiff and shiny. Two little washing machines wait in front of Dieter's appliance repair shop— the steps down to his basement are swamped with drifting snow. Snow surrounds the bare bushes at the deserted construction site, snow tops the bags of garbage piled around the base of a streetlamp. His hands are cold, his keys are cold. Newspapers sit in front of the door to his building, inside a damp smell in the entryway and wet footprints on the linoleum. Fifty-eight stairs, snow on his shoes. The doormat in front of his apartment, the door, finally. The foyer. Everything is good. He kneels on the floor, out of breath. He's sweating. Steam wafts out of the kitchen. Home. *Don't move, don't worry, you are being taken home.* Home. Mama. *Baba.* His knees on the ground, solid ground, breathing in his head, panting in his ears. He wants to stand up and head into the kitchen. He can't. He's jolted from his dream. Suddenly he feels the ropes, feels the gravity. He gasps for breath. He hears himself, alone, a heavy clump somewhere on the face of the earth.

The numb flesh has opened its eyes again. The pain forces it to see. Every blink of the eye hurts. Bowed spine, vertebrae wrenched out of place, pulled muscles. His torso is grotesquely warped, his elbows stick into his gut, his bound wrists are stuck in his crotch. His hands feel far apart from one another and his fingers are numb. Part of his ass is sticking out, the half-domes clenched. The waistband of his pants digs into his cheeks. The material of the crotch, too far down, stretches between his thighs. His feet are crossed, his ligaments pulled, the bottoms of his feet stretched, the Achilles tendon on one foot pressed in, the heel of his other foot lodged in his buttocks. The weight of his entire body, this bundle of contorted limbs, rests on his knees. And on top of the bundle, his head. He can picture it but doesn't want to. It's the head of an insect, with no face. Suckers strapped on tight. Hood, goggles, sound-proof headphones, face mask: false eyes, false ears, strapped to a false head—an alien. He wants out. But he's confined to his skull, no way forward and no way back. Just enough space to breathe.

Inside his head the silence is deafening. He can't avoid hearing his own body. His throat rattles, his tongue clicks, hitting his gums, spittle gurgles between his teeth. He feels the hole in the row, the fresh crater left by his molar. It smacks and rubs, much too close, much too loud, and knocks and whirs, too—like the sound of machinery. He can't block the sounds out. He holds his breath. But the rushing noises continue, the dull hammering. There's no way to stop it. The motor coughs, the machine in his head, it breathes, hisses and pops. His mouth is a sticky cavern; behind it, the narrow passage of his throat. His tongue, a pocked sensor, creeps along the cavern walls, feeling for bumps and holes. When he swallows saliva, the air passage to his lungs closes with a click and then clicks back open. His lungs pump constantly, sucking in air, pushing it out, pausing, starting again. The shallow breaths flow in hot, flow out hot, always the same, never enough. The inflows and outflows swirl together and con-jure up places and images only to blow away names, so that nothing gets in and nothing out, everything trapped in this closed system, this simmering pressure cooker.

Home. He rages, he runs, he tries to figure out where to go on this journey in his mind. Images race by, so many fragments, snow in Hamburg, darkness in Peshawar. In between, the first stop: *Ladies and gentlemen, welcome to Delhi.* He walks down a long jetway. Finally, solid ground beneath his feet, in his nose the smell of rubber and tar. Hot gusts blow between concrete columns. He hears the rolling of thunder and of suitcase wheels, buzzing. His heart skips a beat and his legs tremble; the ground feels like it's shaking. He looks for his grandmother. *Nani.* Fluorescent lights flicker at the end of the corridor. His *Nani* is waiting in the entrance hall. He has a picture of her in his hand and now there she is, waving at him. She's tall and her sari is the same bright blue as in the photo. He recognizes her glasses and the way she has her hair up, thick and white with streaks of black. She laughs and cries. Outside, the evening is warm. Taxi, taxi. Air streams in, leaden air, the taxi's grille plows through the masses. The sidewalks are teeming with people, but the courtyard is empty. The stairs creak. There are flowers on the landing, flowers in the hallway, flowers on the balcony. He sits down on a cushion, his grandfather looking down on him from the wall. *Dada,* says *Nani.* She doesn't speak German or English. Loud activity outside the window all night, the voices of Old Delhi. He sweats under the sheets. Then it's daytime. He sits up, squatting on his knees. Sun dapples his hands, his hands on his knees, his knees on the carpet. It's quiet, just faint murmurs. It's past noon. Colorful sounds rise from the alleyway, bounce around the balcony, linger behind the half-drawn blinds, and seep in through the cracks. A ray of light shines across the red-on-red pattern of the carpet, a transparent column of light slicing through the room, dust and flies dancing in it, up and down against the field of red. His eyes dance with them while his hands are still. A fly lights on his hand. The carpet pattern twinkles. His hands are moist. In the next room a shadow moves. He feels the movement in the air and hears a rustle—and a voice, too. *Nani* is humming: *Rashid, bacha, samufar.* Still on his knees, he rises up off his heels, letting his hands drop. Without standing up, he places two pieces of kindling into the little wrought iron stove beneath the kettle. *Chai,* tea for his tongue, his parched throat, warmth in the heat. He squats back down on his heels. The samovar is coming to a boil. Wisps of steam rise from the shadows into the ray of light casting a thin veil over the carpet. Now there's a soft clatter and *Nani* comes in. His eyes down, he sees her little brown foot step onto the red carpet, her heel landing in the middle of a medallion before shiny fabric, cool blue, sweeps over and covers it. It smells of wet leaves, flower pots and the soil under her fingernails. The edge of her sari brushes him, sending a tingle, like the legs of a fly, from his hairline down to the seam of his collar. *Nani* kneels beside him: in a single motion she glides to the floor and sets a tray with tea glasses down on the carpet. She turns to the samovar. It hisses as a drop of tea falls into the embers and steams off, the flickering embers glinting on a tea glass and *Nani's* eyeglasses. He's thirsty. He reaches out his hand. He can almost feel the smooth surface of the glass cup's metal handle touching his fingertips. But his hand is stuck to his knee. He strains. There's a burning in his arms and shoulders. But his hands are numb. His fingers are a dull mass, bent, stiff and sweaty. His tongue feels gluey. The hem of the sari is still brushing his back, now as sharp as a knife blade. One arm strains against the other, his knees grind into the carpet. There are knots in the pattern, and pins and needles shoot into the bottoms of his feet.

He sinks further back onto his heels. The ankle chains dig into the bone. He lifts his shoulders and leans his head back and rotates it. Stiff, sticky fabric rubs his skin. He can't stop it—it scratches, scrapes, and burns. The hood sits on his skull, his bare skull, like an enormous warm hand. Fine rivulets of sweat run down his neck. His shoulders shiver as the sweat trickles. He longs for the warm pulse of a shower, fear creeping up the back of his neck. New fear, a new batch of images. He is standing naked beneath a pale, green, ringing bell. The flight is over. They have yet to shave his head, but his clothes are gone—the jeans with the ripped knee, stinking and wet, the t-shirt and the sneakers. The wall in front of him is white. Behind him are men in green aprons with masks on and their hands in white rubber gloves. Hoses hiss and shouts reverberate: *Don't move, don't move, go-go-go.* The air is damp and filled with a noxious chemical smell, a bathroom smell. His feet skid on the slippery green tiles, and beneath the soles of his feet he can feel vibrations— everywhere dirty bare feet, slime, suds. He looks down at his legs. The hair on his stomach is stuck to his skin, his ball sac hangs limp, his arms are hidden. Naked bodies flop all around the tiles, exhausted, filthy male bodies. The one beside him is very young; his thin body twitches, he kicks, the hissing gets louder, becomes screeching, and the boy screams. The screeching of the hoses is head-splitting. Steam makes it hard to breath, burns his throat, harsh like ammonia. The boy next to him is small and brown, his back hunches as darts of water hail down on his neck, nee- dle-like stings, needles everywhere, piercing, caustic, fresh, the shower, finally. He gasps, breathless, water hammering his shoulders, his back and sides, he screams. Jets of water burn between his butt cheeks, he laughs, he shouts, his lips burn, his tongue burns, his eyes burn: *Shut up, shitheel, shut up.* The boy beside him has slipped and fallen. With his hands bound behind his back he lies limbless in the suds like a fish. Nobody helps him up. He pushes himself around the floor, kicking his feet like a tail fin, howling. Screams all around, reverberating echoes, each wave fainter and more distant than the last. The tiled room dis- appears, the green fades to white, the images dissipate in the mist.

Squatting on his knees he peers through the fog. All

he can see is the boy. He's forgotten everything else. He gulps, dreams, kneels beside the boy. An unknown boy, a boy like him, bound like him, lying on the floor, he's fallen and injured himself, his knees are shot. He knows him, he wants to help him. Poor kid, struggling on his back, pushing with his legs, trying to find his hands, straining against the handcuffs. His knees are shattered, his feet beat against the tiles, he howls and pants, breathing way too deep, way too fast. Stop that. He tells him. You're hurt. Settle down. Those are just straps around your wrists, needles in your knees, a mask on your face. Now breathe, slowly, deep breaths. In. Out. That's it. Good. You're just in shock. Thin air can knock you out. Stupid boy. The green aprons, they're cleaning women, nurses, and doctors. They've got you. Hang in there, it doesn't hurt. Your knees are shot. You fell over. They grabbed you, took you away, all tied up. You're dazed, stunned, and deaf and blind. Yes, your knees are swollen, your feet bound together. But they're not going to do anything to you. They've tied you up, wrenched your feet, caused your knees to swell up, bound your arms, bagged your head, put a mask on your face. Listen to your breathing, breath steady. See, it's over. Quiet now, easy. *Don't move, don't worry.* The green aprons will take care of you, cradle you, love you. Let yourself be gently rocked, let yourself drift off. Wrapped up tightly in white bandages, a needle draining your knees, tubes in your mouth and nose. They'll look after you, a white bundle, swaddled, packed in and covered, quietly lulled to sleep. You're doing well. You dream, you don't wake. Curled up, you hang from the tube, breathing in and out through your snorkel, watched carefully in a deep sleep.

He slowly slumps to the side. He can't fall over— the strange balance holds him in place. He talks to himself, encouraging himself. His voice sounds distant. His lips move. He takes himself away, far away. He's off traveling again and images glide past like postcards: a furry yak, a wooden bridge over a ravine, a sea of clouds, a barren slope and the steep steps to a toy temple. The second station. Delhi is behind him. In front of him the Himalayas. He sits there, a *Lonely Planet* guide in his lap, shadows beneath the colorful terraced roofs, sun flashing strobe-like through the spokes of rickshaw wheels, and a sign—*Katmandu Trekking Tours*—gleaming on the street corner. The same name is on the side of a bus making its way up the street toward the pass, tourists and backpacks on the seats, dust on the windows. A blue puddle glistens in the distant barren uplands, seemingly at the end of the world, and beyond is the white peak. He's going to take another shot at climbing the mountain, the highest on earth. They climb out of the bus. The air is thin. The trail is steep and rocky. In front is the Nepalese guide, carrying a heavy load, a bowling-pin-shaped basket swaying back and forth above his two sweatpant-clad legs. Backpacks stick out of the basket and on top there's a tarp and ropes. Behind him is the row of climbers. Roped one after the other they trudge along, trekkers with caps, earmuffs, and sunglasses with protective nose pieces. Insect heads on swaying bodies. The sherpa waves his thin arms, pointing to the white cliff. Snow cushions their steps. It's cold and peaceful. He follows the trail in sturdy boots, new jeans, looking down at the rip on his right knee. Suddenly everything is distorted, the rip expands, the snow gets deeper and the trail steeper, his breath shorter. He wants to get to the top—he just needs to keep going, one breath after another, one step after another, despite his heavy feet, heavy knees, roped to the others, tied on securely. The snow shimmers and the air is cold. Faint, lost voices. He whispers to himself. You'll be there soon. Take your time or you'll fall. Keep it together, don't look to the side. Breathe slowly, the air is thin. One step after the other all the way to the roof of the world. White light, dark glasses, eyes down on your feet, your sturdy boots. Keep going, keep going. Step in the footprints of the person in front of you. Bend your knees. Lift your feet. Don't wake up. The journey in your head, shadows in the brilliant white light, sleepwalking along the precipice.

He kneels and breathes, disoriented. Faults of the earth. Deep dream. Slowly he climbs to the top of the ridge, trudging along at the end of the rope, step by step, to the right a sheer cliff, to the left a snowy wasteland. He struggles, tries to keep his balance. His shadow, the legs foreshortened, trudges alongside him, his shadow also lifting its feet, bending its knees, gliding across the white expanse without leaving a trace. He breathes in and out slowly, a breath for every step, and lifts his head to look at the peak. The horizon starts to spin, the mountain tops dip. He crouches down and pauses, quivering. To the left, dark apparitions appear against the white ground. To the right gapes the abyss, the endless depths. He looks down into it. It makes him dizzy, he wheels and suddenly falls over and disappears. Only his shadow remains behind, filling the deep hole in the snow. His body sinks. He's lost his balance. He's fallen. He's crashed. There he lies, tangled up in a ball, buried in the endless white. His eyes are full of snow, snow plugs up his ears. His mouth and nose are snowed in. He swallows snow. He breathes snow. He coughs, wheezes. He writhes in a bundle, buried alive. The sherpa waves from the roof of the world, farther and farther away. Way up high, the line of tiny figures. They climb, they laugh, puffs of breath wafting in front of their mouths. The bundle is stuck, no longer kicking and wriggling. He slumps to the ground. It's hard and crushes his knees. The pain jerks him back. The mountains disappear. He's kneeling on the floor, motionless, hands tied, feet crossed and bound, his senses cut off. He is alive and awake.

The dream is over. All that's left is the ground and his knees, jammed into the ground, battered flesh, bowed bones, a contorted, misshapen mass. He leans to one side but it's impossible for him to fall over. His thighs cramp. The leg irons press into his ankles. His upper body presses on his thighs, his thighs press on his knees, his knees press on the ground, one leg presses into his butt, and the other into the ground. He doesn't dare move. He must wait, breathe, wait, breathe. His weight is poorly distributed, and from weight comes pain, meaning the pain is poorly distributed, as well. There's too much pain in his knees, too little in his feet. Just don't move. His feet hurt, but his knees hurt more. His knees fight his feet, his feet fight his knees. It's a battle over the position of his thighs and butt, where all the weight is. It's a decisive struggle: shift the weight, yes or no, distribute the pain, yes or no. The battle intensifies but neither side is winning. There's no help, no eyes to cry, no mouth to scream, no hands to wring. His knees scream. His feet scream. The battle quickly spreads, from knees to thighs, from heels into hips. His shoulders tense and his arms tear at each other. His lungs pump, the machine continues to pulse, the mask fills with hot, humid air. Then his body makes a decision. His thighs pull fiercely away from each other, the crotch of his pants resisting, the cloth holding them together. His legs shake. Gravel grinds into his knees and they revolt, but they hold up. His haunches weigh ever more on his feet, the weight presses down on his calves, and the stones bore deeper into his feet. The pain is wrong, the decision is wrong. His feet scream, his knees scream, everything screams. It's never quiet. No one hears it, nobody is there. He's alone. He pants. He kneels on the ground. He has arrived, somehow, somewhere. He has to find out how and why, has to search, here on the ground.

The ground is hard. He's breathing fast. Slowly, slowly. He tries to remember. He must know where he is. *Don't move, don't worry, you are being taken home.* Home. He's arrived someplace, on an airplane, in the dark. He listens, he thinks back, trying to remember the last flight, a blind flight, with no destination and no view, just noise in his head, engine noise. One plane flew from Hamburg to Delhi, to *Nani*. One flew from Delhi to Katmandu. Then another flight back to Delhi, with Mirgul, and the train to the Pakistani border. Mirgul the Afghani, Mirgul with his prayer rug, Mirgul from the *Guest House* in Katmandu. The bus has crawled back down the mountain. The room is cheap. His backpack sits next to his bed. He's tired. His bones hurt from the descent. He looks out of the window at the terrace below, feels the thin, cold air. A carpet lies on the stone floor, small, rectangular, with a green and white pattern around the edges. Next to it are a pair of shoes, and before it a boy. The boy, in a blue ankle-length tunic, kneels down on the rectangular carpet, first keeping his upper body straight and his hands on his thighs, then leaning forward and putting his hands on the ground. His rear end hovers above the soles of his feet. His forehead knocks against the ground. Rashid closes the window and goes to sleep. There is more knocking, knocking at the door, *good morning mister.* Lying on the mattress, he can feel a draft as the door cracks open. A strip of blue material appears in the partially open doorway, a white patch stitched to it, and above a broad face, smiling, showing teeth and bluish gums. It's the boy, standing in the corridor. There's a tooth missing from his smile, and he has a splotch on his forehead, a gray-blue lump on his brown skin. The door opens the rest of the way, a beam of light comes in, and now he can see the prayer rug rolled up under the boy's arm. Without even thinking about it, Rashid looks for the pattern on the carpet. The boy understands. He steps into the room, unrolls the carpet on the bare floor, points to himself, the rug, and then the mattress: *Mimirgul, mislam, mister?* The melody of his speech fills the room, the rising tone at the end directed at him. He sits up, pulls up his knees. On the left knee is a rip in the expensive new jeans he'd bought just for this trip, bought on Grosse Bergstrasse in Hamburg, along with the cheap t-shirts from Woolworth's, and the sun block and bug spray from the drugstore. *Me Mirgul, me Islam, you good, America good.* He looks at the boy and shakes his head: *I am Rashid, no American, no mister.* The boy smiles, the gap in his teeth showing at the side of his mouth. *You good, you brother, you wror.* He motions to the door. *You come, you breakfast.* His feet are bare. He's wearing pants under his tunic. He disappears into the hallway, leaving the light streaming into the room. *You come.* Rashid stands up. The boy in Katmandu, the boy with the *Room Service Tibet Guest House* patch on his tunic, the same boy next to him on the airplane on the way back to Delhi, *wror*, his brother Mirgul with the canvas duffel bag. *You come with me. Family in Pakistan. Parents in Afghanistan. War is over.* The train station in Delhi is a mob scene. Strips of bright morning light slash across the white platform beneath the impossibly lofty roof. His backpack leans against a steel support beam. Mirgul sits on top of it, right in the middle of the throngs, his prayer rug rolled up under his arm. He laughs, waves his tattered visa, and they fight their way onto the train, pushing and pulling. It's hot, animals, baskets, sweat and dust everywhere. Amritsar station in the afternoon, dragging themselves through the alleyways, the golden temple glittering in the reflection pool. Mirgul doesn't have any money. The taxi drives through fields of wheat. Then they're at the border, waiting all night for their passports and their bus tickets. *Welcome to Pakistan.* Morning in Lahore, another bus, this one full of sleeping men, their heads swaying back and forth in their seatbacks. Outside barren highlands and the cities, Rawalpindi, Islamabad. He dreams, he continues his journey, getting ever closer. It's cold in Peshawar, the bus station, Khyber street, the Saddar bazaar, Storyteller street. Mirgul speaks in English, in Pashtun, asking the way to Kharkhana. A taxi drives through the mud toward the corrugated iron shacks of Little Afghanistan. *War is over.* Mirgul asking questions and gesturing, jumping out of the car, stopping people to ask them. Finally the shack, a shack full of sleeping bags and people, Mirgul's aunt, Mirgul's brother, his friends, his old *Ana.* The trip is over, and soon the moment of truth. The shack is in Kharkhana; the women pack. The garage is in the city; the men work on the truck. Everyone talks of Jalalabad, of Kabul. The truck has to be able to make it over the pass. *War is over.* One day left, the last day in Peshawar, with its streets full of merchants, full of refugees, men in turbans, men with beards, more and more men, a mob, screams, batons, and he's lying face down in the mud without his passport, his visa, without anything—everything gone, the shack, Mirgul, the *Ana.* Everything goes black. He tries to figure out the final stage, that last flight. He's getting closer. He hears voices in Urdu, Pashtun, voices in a basement, a basement full of men, cold and dark. Then a door opens, finally a light, uniforms, brown and camouflaged, and new voices: *Head down, don't move, shut up, go-go-go.*

He's close now. The voices stop and the light disappears. Keep going, keep going, he has to figure it out. But the weight keeps him from moving forward. The ball of limbs is too heavy, he's staked to the ground, shins and heels crossed over one another, a hard bundle of tendons stretched to the breaking point. The load bears down on the stumps at the end, his knees, pressing his crossed legs into the ground in the shape of an X. His body slumps beneath its own weight, but there's no give at the base, his crossed legs, which hold up even though they can't bear the weight. They want to bend and flex and stretch, straighten out, uproot themselves from the ground, soften the earth. But the earth stays hard. The pressure keeps pressing. The weight keeps bearing down. The earth comes to life, holding its ground, pushing back against his body. It secretes tiny bubbles which harden and multiply, pressing into the surface: Gravel, nettles, buds, thorns. Sharp edges battle dull. Sprouts shoot out, break through, push up, bore their way into his skin, stab into his feet, shins, knees. The ground is winning. Suddenly he understands—the earth is taking over his body. The tips are already implanted in his kneecaps. They're expanding inside and branching out, a thrusting, climbing vine, farther and farther, higher and higher. Fine stems cleave their way up through muscles, bore holes through bones. Stalks wind themselves around his thighs and arms, pull themselves up his limbs, climb his spine. The dense brush draws sustenance from the ground, burrows through his body tissue, spreads, divides, sends out branches. The farthest tendrils push back outwards, straining against the retaining wall of his skin. They bunch up and wind upon themselves before continuing to grow further. Pustules start to pop out of his skin. He twitches. He clenches up. He tries to stop it. But they burst one after the other. He feels it. He sees it. He watches as the tendrils drive their way out of his skin. The stalks push through, his skin rips, hanging in strips from the branches. One splinter after the next pops out and shoots upward. The ball of limbs melts, its insides pushed out, all its strength squeezed out, red, bright red, spurting, pumping, beating and beating, exploding into the open. A flood streams in from outside now—he hears the mob, smacks, feet stomping. He sees the demonstrators, fists flying, graying clerics and brown uniforms, boots in the mud. Mud on the streets of Peshawar. *War is over.* Boots in his face, his face in the mud. His face still stuck in the mud.

He can't breathe. The pain is suffocating him. He starts from the beginning again. This is the floor. These are his knees. This is his neck, he can swivel it. This is his head. Easy now. Nice and easy. He concentrates on the voices from Peshawar in his head. First there's the rhythm, the stomping, clapping, and beating of an angry march through the muddy streets. There are robes, beards and turbans dancing, and fists and scarves dancing with them. Banners, turquoise flags, sleeves falling down up-stretched arms, the pages of Korans fluttering, a carnival crowd. Everyone chants in unison: *jihad, jihad.* The voices of the clerics call out prayers: *Allahu akbar, death to America, marg bar Amrika.* Along the sides of the street—under awnings and up on balconies—are women and children. Puffs of breath are visible in front of the mouths shouting *marg bar Amrika.* Suddenly whistles and sirens, screams scurry all around. The men run, their tunics fluttering behind them, stiff uniforms running after them. Blows rain down. He falls to the ground. Arms on his back. His face in the mud. Right in front of his face a black boot sinks into the deep mud. The toe is splattered with mud. Above it a brown pant leg with a crisp crease. A blow, a rip, and then darkness. He's sitting in a basement. The back of his head is leaning against the wall; someone else's head is on his shoulder, asleep. He's been locked up. He listens. Rustling, laughing, squeaking, rats in a basement in Peshawar. His arm has fallen asleep. He listens to the voices of the other prisoners: *ya Allah*. Echoes reverberate in the invisible space. He waits for light and feels around in the dark. Dry mud on his clothes. The oily, bristly hair from the head leaning on his shoulder scratches at his neck. It's cold. His bladder is full. His shoulders are numb. Snoring, murmurs. *Ya Allah*. The head leaning on his shoulder slides down into the crook of his arm but the man doesn't stir. The floor is cold and hard, and sharp smells rise from it—piss and sweat, the sweat scented with tea, cumin and cardamom. The head cradled in his elbow moves as the man twitches in his sleep. Sighs, scraping, faint cries. Bodies everywhere. *Marg bar Amrika, marg bar Amrika.* He tries to remember. He waits in the dark. Eventually, the basement will have to be opened. He waits for the inevitable beam of light, the uniforms, the boots, the new voices, the familiar language, *hands up, head down*, the camouflaged soldiers in Peshawar. The beginning is still missing, the beginning of the end, the last stage of his journey.

Everything is black. Only the pain flares up like spontaneous brush fires or shots from an unseen sniper. He can't seem to find the way out, the way he got here. He just can't figure it out. He wants to give up and sink into the earth, heavy as he is, this lump, this nonentity. He exhales hard—pushing the air out, emptying his lungs, his rib cage sinking into his body—gathering his strength, clenching the pain. A piercing sound blares in his head, he sees stars, his throat croaks, crushing pressure kicks in and he gives in. His lungs suck in air and the mask presses against his nose and lips. His blood rushes, pounding in the silence. The stars dancing before his eyes expand and merge. He rocks and sways. The pain washes out over him like a hot lake, and the dizziness lifts him up above the fiery surface. He floats. He peers down. Below is a shapeless lump, without definition, without a face, without a name. *What is your name?* The voice is very close, sharp and clear. He remembers. The voice belongs to the pair of light brown boots just below his blinded eyes. Camouflage pants rise from the tops of the boots. He lifts his head. The basement has been opened. The beginning is here.

The room is small, a hole in the ground. He kneels on the damp ground, hands behind his back. *Why did you come to Peshawar?* The soldier is sitting on an earthen bench cut into the dirt wall. Another one is standing against the wall. *Why did you want to go to Afghanistan?* He understands, but he can't speak. He searches for an answer. But they're faster, and they jump up, jerk him up, *go-go-go*. He's thrown in front of a door. It's light outside. They push his head down to his chest. The floor is damp, and in the mud sits a row of men in black hoods, lined up tightly one after the other with their legs collapsed beneath them. *Sit down.* He sits and then disappears into a black hole. The hoods are sacks, yanked down over the head. Knees and forehead pressed to the man in front of him, waiting in the dark, cold wetness seeping through the bottom of his pants. The final journey is beginning, the journey in his head. First there's noise, engine noise. He's being pulled up, crammed in, shoved between soft bodies and hard beams. Then he's on the ground again, the sound of propellers, commands, *get up, lift your feet.* Squinting, gasping for air, he sees his own bare feet in the sticky, wet, canvas sneakers, and the barrel of a rifle in his chest. He is standing in front of a sheet metal wall on a concrete floor, a gutter running along the edge of the wall. Soldiers are taking the sacks off the heads of the men beside him. They shout as they untie their hands as well. Their voices reverberate: he is to piss in the gutter, he is to eat the bread out of the plastic dish they hold in front of him with rubber gloves on—two halves of a double-decker peanut butter sandwich—he is to drink water, he is to swallow two pills, and quick. He senses that the yelling and dry, cracking punches around him have to do with the pills; he slurps them down, drinks, and disappears again under the sack. It's black, completely black, but now he can remember everything. The constricted wrists. The vice-grips on his arms. Stumbling up a shaky staircase, landing with a dull echo on his ass on the slippery metal floor of a tube. His legs stretched out on the metal, cold rings around his ankles, chains attached to the floor. The fear—violent, shivering fear—that spills over him as another ring is drawn across his chest, wrapped around his arms and tightened, as a voice—his own voice—cries out and his upper body starts to shake and lurch in the restraining rings. And the numbness creeping down his neck from the touch of the rough gloves. Beyond the black cloth a voice booms an incantation, an order: *Don't move, don't worry, you are being taken home.* Then something is clamped over his ears, and a whooshing abyss swallows the final sentence. The container his head's been stuffed into begins to buzz and vibrate, then to bang, all the noises layering on top of each other. It's too much. The container starts to squash his head, to cut it off from his body. His body slips over the edge and falls, falling without ever touching down, falling and falling.

He is still slowly falling, inert. He has long since broken through the earth's crust and sunken in, his knees leading the way. Sprouts have ripped through the cloth, driven into his kneecaps and permeated his flesh, which burrows further into the depths, layer after layer. The weight pulls him down with it, matter merging with matter. It's getting hotter. Ever more willingly the earth yields, getting softer and opening up, sucking and voracious—a shallow impression becomes a pit, a pit becomes a crater, a crater becomes a chasm. The foundation has already melted, his toes dissolved, his hands disintegrated. On the ground is a crude bundle with blurry edges. Its porous shell is falling away, tattered ligaments crumble into white tufts and mix with the surrounding earth. His bodily fluids seep from his carcass into the whitish sludge. It rises, ever whiter and chalkier; chalk fills the chasm, stringy like rubber. The pressure forces his arms together, warps his backbone. The cloth between his thighs fuses with the limp muscles, his rear and hips collapse. The chasm is filling in and closing up. The soil creeps up over his shoulders and neck to his head. His throat burns, his eyes are sealed shut, his ears fill up. His head is a lump without a skull. In front of the air holes the ventilation bag inflates. Air is still flowing in and out of the mask, sucking and exhaling weakly, waiting to suffocate. The last breath echoes in his stopped up ears and a sound rings out, a droning hum from within the cavernous pit, from the now-buried interior.

On his knees he waits, his limbs bound and his head wrapped. He hums without noticing he's doing so. The journey is wrenching its way to an end. The last airplane. He hangs in rope webbing, rubber straps around his chest and stomach, ice cold, skin wet, numbing darkness. There's the dull roar of engines, piss on his thigh; he rolls around, dazed, freezing. The landing. Rumbles, hissing, falling over. His empty stomach cramps up and there's a choking feeling in his throat. They take off his soundproof

headphones and the stinking, wet hood. Yes, he is alive—
he just doesn't seem to have any hands or feet. The crash
to the ground. They grab him. A blast of hot air and light.
A whole army on the landing strip, sharpshooters, tanks,
military transports. A push and his head smashes onto the
asphalt. The welcome. Vice-grips on his upper arms,
words rattle from unseen faces, a stomping rap: *go-go-go,
shut up, keep your head down.* Everywhere shoes on the
asphalt, worn out sandals, metal chains dragging, rubber
slippers, ankles ripped open by leg-irons, filthy cloth shoes
with worn down heels, sand colored boots with rounded
steel toes. The ride. The ankle chains clank against pol-
ished aluminum bumps, the smell of gasoline, wet bodies
on benches, deep silence except for the humming
engine—the silence of the desert, of death. The ocean. A
shimmering expanse beyond the nose of ship. *Eyes down.*
Swaying and rocking in the dim belly of the ship, the scent
of piss and fuel oil, then again blinding light. *Don't talk,
get up, look down.* The ocean, green and glittering, visible
once again between steel beams. The dream fades with the
ocean at his back—he has arrived.

No. Not here. Not now. He turns around. There's a
ringing in his plugged ears, and time speeds up as the
images reverse and stream backwards. No sooner is he
down on his knees than he's gliding back, blindfolded and
deaf, gravel under his feet, leg irons on, vice-grips on his
arms. Then he's in the dark, and they are putting the
chains on his ankles, pressing his shoulders forward so his
arms can be held together in front of his stomach, wrap-
ping his forearms with duct tape. His hands disappear into
a foam bundle, the goggles' suction cups are stuck onto his
eyes, noise-blocking shells are clapped over his ears, the
face mask is put over his nose and mouth, and a hood is
pulled over his bare skull. Then suddenly he can see and

hear again. The world is bathed in red, flaming reddish orange, and pale green. In an orange suit he kneels on the tiles as fingers in rubber gloves steady his chin. A woman in a white mask and green cap is running clippers through his hair, stripe after stripe, from his temples to the back of his neck, making a dull humming in his skull, buzzing. The buzzing gets louder, he's naked and they're spraying disinfectant and next to him the injured boy jerks around on the wet floor. Now the buzzing is tremendous and the images race by faster, still rewinding—towards home, over the ocean, through wilting heat into black cold, a boat, a truck, an airplane, further and further. He's sitting in a basement, clerics dance in the muddy streets, chants of Allah, a musty shack, hot tea. Mirgul's *Ana* crying, Mirgul sleeping at the border crossing in Wagah, Mirgul laughing during the flight from Katmandu to Delhi, Mirgul sitting on the terrace, the *room service* patch on his tunic, *you come with me, war is over.* Further. He stands there dizzy at the edge of a cliff, wisps of clouds, white silence, waiting on Flick Street in front of *Katmandu Trekking Tours*, sitting on the steps of the temple. He is flying along the Himalayas, the peaks hovering in the oval window. *Nani* hands him a glass of tea, flies dance in the beam of light, noise in the alleyway, a cow pokes its head into a dumpster, the minarets of a mosque tower like giant onions in the sky, *welcome to Delhi*, the coastline shimmers far below. *Don't worry*, take it easy, nice and easy. His head buzzes, he listens, he continues back. Tired at the Hamburg airport, his backpack on the bench in the back of the van with *Baba* at the wheel, snow on Seilerstrasse, steam in the kitchen, light in the hallway, a melody in his ears, very close, getting ever closer. He is swimming in the melody, glittering waves, the voice of the earth. He hears the voice—it's his own. He's a glob of humming flesh. The buzzing builds, it rises, it opens, he screams.

The scream rattles his skull, shreds his throat, pierces his ears and is broken off with a blow. A boot. A kick in the back. The end. He falls on his side, knees free, his head in the gravel. He is here. He's arrived at last. Somewhere on earth, a prisoner, I, Rashid.

II. *Food.* Slop

There's a time each day when the camp is perfectly still. For a long time, Rashid thought it was just a lull in all the noises. As if all the various sources of noise took a little break at the same time—all the voices and footsteps, the distant construction work, the bellowing and whimpering of the dogs, the endless rattling of the chain-link fence, the slurping sound of gravel accompanying the rhythmic clanking of leg irons, even the flapping of the red, white, and blue flag. And before the monotonous whirring sounds stir back to life, you can clearly hear the ocean. What is usually just a steady background sound that bare-ly registers suddenly steps to the fore: a pure, peaceful whoosh.

Only after Rashid had given up trying to count the days and, along with them, the number of times he had been able to hear the ocean, did he figure out the source of the stillness. He was sitting on the ground, lean-ing against the southeast corner of his cage—the only corner he can sit in and stretch out his legs without hitting the mattress—staring at the bottom crossbar of the cage, keeping first one eye open and then the other. Through his left eye the world had a slightly red tinge, in his right eye more of a blue-green hue. Looking at the crossbeam and meshed wire of the wall above it, blinking back and forth between the warmer colors of the one eye and the cooler colors of the other, he realized, feeling slightly dizzy, that something crucial was missing from his field of view. At that same moment he heard the whooshing of the ocean. He closed his eyes and took a deep breath. He could smell water, algae and even fuel oil, like in the harbor. Then a jeep revved somewhere and the sea disappeared, wheels screeched, and time continued. Nearby, rubber sandals shuffled along on concrete and clip-clopped against bare heels. The loudspeaker crackled. Rashid fixed his eyes on the base of the side wall until he saw what he was looking for. From the top edge of the crossbeam, shadows crept onto the inside edge of the beam. Before they had disappeared, shadow diamonds crept onto the outside edge. The sun had just passed its highest point.

Rashid lies on the mattress, the thin, blue plastic blanket on the back of his neck. His pant legs are hiked up to his knees. The shade has made it to his feet. It's so hot he pictures the slanted roof of the cage melting, raining down on him in molten drops until, with burning skin and eyes, he is looking up with nothing between him and the sky. Rashid sits still. Nothing should move—not his body, not his thoughts, not even his ribcage. But his chest does go up and down, and with each breath he sucks in a foul, cesspit odor along with that of harsh but sweetly-scented chemical disinfectants. He tries not to let the smells get too deep into his head, as it's already full of images just waiting to be rinsed away and dumped. There's the staircase covered in worn, red linoleum. The gray rubber toe-molding. The worn-through paint of the court-yard walls. The funny little bathroom windows high up on each floor. There's the smell of old Herr Erxleben's beer shits on the second floor, the overwhelming scent of flowers from the Yucel family on the third floor, and on the fourth floor. . . . In another image that schoolboy sprawls on the tiles as jets of stinging chemical suds are sprayed at him from behind. The boy kicks against Rashid's shins and gasps for air but he's unable to help him. . . . If one of these images fades, there are dozens of others that can come crashing in and press down on him until he himself is down on the ground flailing about. When that happened once before, they took his mattress, sheets, blanket and towel away for the night. They swore if it happened again they'd throw him in an isolation cell. *Iso cell—why not,* he had said over his shoulder to the freckled military policeman as he struggled with the mattress. The other one, who had from outside the cage unhooked the chain temporarily tethering him to the doorframe and pulled it back out through the chain-link fencing, smacked his hand against the fence with a hollow clang and answered: *Don't think you'd like it.*

Don't think you'd like it. Rashid doesn't need any convincing. He doesn't want to remember. He needs to pay attention. Memories are dangerous. They bring time into the cage, and the cage is too small for that. As soon as time has a chance to stretch out it pulls him off in every direction. But he can go only two steps in any direction, two normal strides lengthwise, two small ones across. If he were to let himself go, he'd squash himself against the chain-link walls. So Rashid spends all his time working against the imposition of time. He tries to make sure he's able to block it out with as few interruptions as possible. He can't afford to waste too much energy, either outwards or inwards. Sweating is bad; anything that makes him think about the state of his body is bad. To avoid retaining any extra heat, he stretches his arms out, keeping them away from his body, palms facing up as if he were begging. He has to keep the suit on, though, because of the mosquitoes. The label inside the shirt and pants reads: 65% polyester, 35% cotton, size M.

26

He tries to hold his uvula up in the back of his throat. That way he can breath while filtering the stench. At the same time he keeps his eyes half-closed so his thoughts won't have too much space. What he sees holds his thoughts in check. That way they stay within the steel links and climb around the honeycomb pattern of the fence. Even without the smell of the ocean, the pattern reminds Rashid of fishing nets, hung out in rows to dry. And the razor wire beyond could be a fish weir, the coils just round enough for a man to crawl his way in. The men are the fisherman, fishermen dressed up for Carnival, or perhaps they're the fish, giant goldfish with round backs and long side fins. The rays of the sun get caught in this large-scale net, too, making the wire mesh glitter like silver jewelry. Rashid can't see through the row of cages on the other side of the path because most of the men have hung their sheets on the side facing him in order to block the sun. During the day the MPs don't stop them from doing that. He'd tried it himself once, tying the corners of the sheet to the fencing just under the slanted roof which, on the south side, was an arm's length taller than him but on the north side he had to duck his head to stand under. But as soon as he could no longer look out of the cage he felt as if he were being watched. He felt trapped.

From far away, the white, wrinkled sheets give off an air of gypsy-like disarray, of spontaneity, and so, to recreate this camping atmosphere in his own cage, Rashid had hung his towels—the small one and the large one, which most of them put down on the concrete floor to pray on. He tied them into the fencing of the southwest and southeast corners, where they hung limply as if on a hooks. Looking around, Rashid can see the silhouettes of the see-through cages cast on the tall plywood wall beyond them, the row of cages themselves, the cylindrical buckets, the raised mattresses, the strips of hanging cloth and himself, the shed dweller. Now, lying on the white mattress, he gazes from north to south, looking at the effects of the light, orange figures moving in slow motion. So many peaceful, snow-white towels. *War is over.* The memory bores into his head like a bolt. He pinches his eyes shut, trying to block the pain. He snaps them open again. Goldfish-red blots out the white of his sheets for a second. The restless scraping from the next cage drills into his ears.

War is over. Suddenly he's sure this sentence is where it all began; it's this sentence that has brought him here. Not the adventure-seeking loneliness of the *Tibet Guest House* after the trekking tour. Not Mirgul's goodhearted *wror*, brother, when he met him that morning. Not the excited stories of a family reunion in Peshawar. Not the invitation to Jalalabad that he couldn't turn down because his desire to travel further dovetailed with his desire to be polite. It was the sound of *war is over*, conspiratorial, triumphant, infectious. Everything else was just coincidence, destiny, mistakes—war. He would have gone even if he had known it was a lie. To go where a war had just ended was almost as exciting as going to war. Just not as dangerous. He hadn't been interested in the war anyway. They dropped a few bombs, far from Delhi, far from *Nani*, and hunted in the mountains for a couple of bearded men in kaftans—they were always dropping bombs somewhere and hunting for somebody.

He never could stand the Americans. He had only recently realized why, or at least better understood why, while listening to his parents fight about the Americans. Mama showed sympathy for them, saying it was only right for them to defend themselves. *Baba* said, on the contrary, you had to defend yourself against them, and they should hardly have been surprised when a couple of lunatics who felt that way pushed the envelope too far. He compared them to the English in India, said they were a colonial power, too. Mama said he had forgotten his Gandhi. Gandhi could never accomplish anything against the Americans, he told her: they buy everyone they can't suppress with violence. With that he ripped the stalks off a carrot and tossed the orange root in a box. Rashid was surprised at *Baba's* stubbornness. It was a relief he didn't have to feel sorry for the disgusting people he remembered from his childhood in Mainz. He was always astounded at how much louder than everyone else they were. The Americans he saw on the Reeperbahn in Hamburg were blowhards. So were the ones on TV. Their language was overblown, their movies were overblown, and so were their skyscrapers, their threats, their bombs, and even their sorrow. He had no idea how to say blowhard in English, otherwise he'd have been able to better express himself to Mirgul when he responded to Mirgul's *America good. They are not cool,* he had said to Mirgul. *They kill people but they are no terminators.*

    Now he's sweating. He hadn't been paying attention. His thoughts had run off and he had gone after them. Rustling and chains clanking nearby; Rashid lifts his head and props himself up on his elbows. He knows that the more closed-in he feels, the more systematically he needs to keep looking around. Two green-orange-green trios trudge along in front of the row of cages opposite him, one after the other. In the next cage Tarik has stopped pacing. He is sitting on his heels with his back to Rashid, his knees tucked up under his arms, swaying back and forth. He swats at mosquitoes with his Koran. The cage beyond him is empty, and in the ones beyond that the orange suits are lying on their mattresses in the shadows. *Orangutans* Tarik calls them—and himself with them. Or

just *orangs*. Sometimes *oranges*. *No food,* he had said, gesturing to the figures lying in the cages beyond his. To
make himself clear he had held his right hand in front of
his open mouth and waved with his left. Then he had
swiped his hand across his throat to express how seriously
they meant it. Two old guys on Rashid's other side, toward
the watchtower, are gone. One had been picked up,
motionless, and taken from his cage after he hadn't stood
up for two days. When they stood him upright his legs
couldn't hold his own weight. As he was rolled across the
turf on a gurney, his head, covered in white stubble,
bounced up and down like a deflated ball. The other
one—a wiry guy with a high-pitched voice—is probably
sitting in the *iso cell*. In his stall is a new guy. Rashid knows
his name. Suleyman shouted his name so loudly to him
that he immediately had the angered attention of an MP.
But he just got louder. *Donkey* he screamed at the soldier.
Suleyman's no coward. Surely he will stink, because a
shower has been denied him, and, with 15 minutes out of
his cage per week, he's starting at the lowest rung.

Rashid's shins are burning. The crisscrossed
shadows reach to his knees. With them the sun; they fill
half the cage. The water in the wash bucket at his feet must
be hot by now. He sits up, puts his feet down alongside the
mattress and rolls his pant legs down. The wrinkles stay
in—the cloth is stiff with the bug spray they treat it with.
He looks down at his feet hanging out of the pant legs.
They look different. They're brown except for the white
lines left by his sandals, two lines running diagonally back
from the space between his big toe and the next one.
They're covered with bites and stings. His ankles are
rubbed raw. His toenails are split and frayed. Twice he's
tried to soften his feet in the water bucket and carefully rip
out hangnails. The soles of his feet absorb the lukewarm

heat of the concrete floor. It's a soothing sensation, as is looking at the shifting color of the shadow patterns in parts of the cage, alternating between bright gray-white and coal black. He doubles over, feeling nauseous; the stench has rooted in his belly. He takes a sip of water from the olive drab rubber flask and tries to picture the warm fluid running into his stomach and gushing out with the gases. But the gurgling in his gut is drowned out. Heavy, crunching steps: the guy with the red face and the fat black guy. The shadows of their heads move across the sunny patch, across the water bucket and the towels. Too late. Too many people out and about. He'll never get an escort before prayers. There's not enough time to unlock the cage, put him in a *three-piece*—belt, handcuffs and leg irons—to go to the latrine; to undo the handcuffs; to put them back on for the walk back, remove all the chains and lock up the cage again. He had lost track of time. Rashid takes another sip of water and screws the top back on. The two MPs lock up a cage to his right, three down from Tarik, where one of the hunger strikers is lying.

Diagonally across from him, opposite the cage door, is where he keeps the flask, in front of the waste bucket. He had struggled with where to keep the two white buckets. The northeast corner gets the least sun. So it should be the coolest spot in the cage. And besides that it's also on the side away from the path, so it's farthest from the view of the soldiers. In order to put the waste bucket in that corner, he had to put the water bucket in the opposite corner, diagonally across the cage. This kept the clean stuff as far away as possible from the dirty, but it meant the clean water bucket sat in the heat of the southwest corner. It also meant the waste bucket was right next to the head of his mattress. If he had to piss at night, Rashid would then put the waste bucket in the southeast corner of the cage until morning. You got punished if you pissed through the fence. Using buckets of the same color means they can use them for either function. Every evening the used buckets are swapped for disinfected new ones. The one with water in it could be the one another prisoner crapped in the night before. Who knows—it could even be his own waste bucket. He worries about the moment he'll have to cover the bucket with the washcloth he has hanging on the side of the cage next to the hand towel. At the moment the only things in the waste bucket are orange peels and egg shell from breakfast. He had to hand back the plastic plate from lunch along with the plastic spoon with short tines cut into the end that they call a *spork*. This morning, while it was still cool, he had eaten the cream-cheese covered roll—*bagel* they say—under the flood-lights. He had let the cornflakes soften in the milk, stirring them around until they were soft like cream of wheat. At lunch he had eaten the brown lentils and all the dry stuff as well—peanuts, raisins, chips, sesame sticks. When he's eating he forgets about time. He stuffs it in, dry, dull, unsalted time. He chews it slowly and thoroughly and swallows it. At first he had eaten too fast. He chewed hurriedly and shoved in the candy bar afterwards. He'd barely gotten a bite into his mouth before he had another one ready to go—one in his mouth and one in his hand. Afterwards he'd been ashamed. He tossed the remnants into the waste bucket and then sat there waiting for the next meal. The time he'd saved by eating so quickly rolled toward him in a heavy, indigestible lump, just like the one he felt in his stomach. He wished he could fish it out with a soup spoon.

Over time he's gotten fat. His body is soft and limp. As if to protect him, his body has enclosed itself in its own form of captivity. The belt to which the handcuffs and leg irons are always attached no longer encounters the hard resistance of the early days. When two MPs stand on either side of him and grab the reddish brown leather belt in their fists and pull it tight at his back, it digs into a layer of flab that seems separate from his body. With his eyes trained on the ground, he can see the orange suit bunched up around the belt like flesh that's been cut away from his belly. If he tries to look up, away from his cinched body, whoever has his hand on his back reaches up and pushes his head back down to his chest. His shoulders are crumpled forward anyway and his chest caved in because the metal rings locking his hands to his body are so low they won't allow an upright stance. The other guard grabs his upper arm; those muscles don't hold up under the practiced, violent pressure anymore either. His calves shake with the stress of lifting his feet, able to take only one tiny step at a time because of the short, heavy chain of the leg irons.

In threes to the latrine, to the yard, to the showers. Always wedged between, always entrusted to the intricate, brutal tenderness of the bodyguards. Their selfless care reminds Rashid of EMTs, good Samaritans, firemen. They put up with things and suffer, but they're strong. They keep an eye on each other. They yowl like dogs on short leashes in their pinched drawl, which the prisoners awkwardly imitate. Their kindness they leave behind in some building on the far side of the camp. Their names they cover up with green or black tape stuck over the patches above their chest pockets. They are machines and they function perfectly—when they see red, they're rough, hard, goal-oriented, ready to kill if they have to. They know exactly what the bodies under their care need to survive. They're just as good with the ways to break a body, subjugate it, humiliate it. They are military policemen working barn duty, giants in green and brown camo, black boots and tall military caps, experts in human mannerisms. They're human, of that much Rashid is sure. There are even women among them; it hurts to see them, to hear them, to be touched by them. The old man next to him always turns his back as soon as he sees a woman coming and hides his face in his hands. He gets enraged whenever he is supposed to be escorted anywhere by one. Once after he spat at one of them he disappeared for a while. Their voices come from higher up in their bodies, nearer their hearts, there where their breasts are beneath their uniforms. It makes the sound even more piercing when they yell, order, or ask questions: *What's up? What now?* Tarik always shouts *woman* to them, but they don't react, they just walk off even faster, as if they were being followed. The young pretty one with a ponytail cinched up near the rim of her cap, the only white one, finally couldn't keep herself from responding one morning while passing out breakfast, and said: *You have to call me MP, if not you'll lose recreation time.* After that Tarik stopped calling her *woman* and started calling her *Call-me-MP*. She's the only MP Rashid has ever seen smile. One night Rashid woke up to the sound of a hushed conversation and looked over and saw her in front of Tarik's cage. As he shifted, Tarik looked around warily. Rashid closed his eyes. His heart beat madly with jealousy. He heard Tarik whisper: *I mean, your boy, he touch you always? What do you mean, always,* she asked. *I mean, if you*—Tarik lowered his voice even more—*if there is blood, you know.* They were both silent for a strained moment, until she asked: *Is it banned in your country?* Tarik: *Yes, It's not good. It's not clean. I mean, it's not the want of Allah.* Rashid heard her sigh. *I won't blame your Allah,* she said. *Sleep now.* Then her footsteps crunched past Rashid's cage.

Now Tarik is standing at the fence, fingers hooked into the chain-links, watching what's going on three cages down. The door is open and the black MP is leaning over the orange suit. Apparently they've tied him up lying down. The white MP speaks into his walkie-talkie. It sounds like code numbers. The men in adjacent cages and on the opposite side of the path start to move. The ones lying down sit up and the ones sitting down stand up. The white MP is getting louder. *Stretcher*, he shouts into the walkie-talkie. *Infirmary.* He ducks his head and enters the cage. He lifts a bucket, looks into it, shakes it. He puts it down. He walks back out. Rashid presses against the fence of his cage. All the oranges are pressed up against the fences. They all turn their heads towards Mecca, towards the tower they know from recreation time. It's wooden, with machine guns on the covered parapet and an American flag painted on the side. The sound of footsteps comes from that direction, people running and wheels grinding. The tall blond MP is rolling the gurney. His shadow is as tall as he is and it passes through the cages. As he goes by Rashid can see beads of sweat beneath the bill of his cap.

The sun is low in the sky, wringing out its last drops of heat. The commotion can't impede the peace descending. The shadows in his cage have nearly reached the waste bucket. Now they're heaving the limp body onto the gurney. The orange cloth gets caught and they have to lift the body a couple of feet above the surface of the gurney before they can free it and set him down. The blond MP holds the gurney steady. Rashid can feel the lentils in his stomach expanding and the pressure of gas in his intestines. He squats next to the fence, hooks his fingers into the chain links and leans back with outstretched arms. He grunts as he stretches, trying to relieve the feeling in his stomach. Tarik turns around in his cage, gestures to the commotion in the cage beyond, and puts his pointer finger into his open mouth. He's trying to indicate a feeding tube being inserted into the stomach, but it makes Rashid think of the sign for puking. He stares at his knees trying to suppress the queasiness. *Hospital,* Tarik says. The blond MP comes back past, in each hand a white bucket. He swaggers by them, casting a sideways glance as Tarik yells at him. *Now eat,* Tarik says, grinning. They watch the camo-clad MP walk away. As if to finalize the departure, Tarik smacks a mosquito in his neck. The whole thing is nearly done. The black MP secures the gurney as the other one locks up the cage, then he positions himself in front. He pulls, the white MP pushes. Gravel squirts out from under the wheels. Rashid presses his face to the gate of his cage. First his view is filled with the massive body of the MP, hunched over the gurney. Then he can see the back of the head of the prisoner. He must have been one of the first in, because his hair has grown back to an inch or so in length. Just as the gurney goes past Rashid, his head rolls and he sees two black eyes, wide open, staring out of deep sockets. Except for his fists—handcuffed, lying in his lap—and his feet—which dangle over the edge of one corner of the stretcher—his body is as flat as an empty set of orange clothes just laid out on the bed. The measly load disappears behind the back of the white MP, just an orange strip receding into the distance.

The path is empty. But the men in the stalls are restless. They hang up their sheets, grab their washcloths, shift their buckets around, roll up their sleeves and pant legs, wind towels around their heads. Tarik squats in front of his water bucket. He bends over it, dips his hand in, sticks his wet pointer finger in his ears, brings his cupped hands to his face, snorts water into his nose, spits out through the fence. He runs his wet hands over his head. He washes his feet standing up, balancing himself on one foot and then the other, leaving each sandal in place on the floor. He reaches out, his hand shimmying along the fencing, and grabs the big towel. He stands on the balls of each feet and rolls his pant legs down. Then he puts each arm in the bucket, washing them to the elbow, and dries them. He never uses the liquid soap.

Ever more white turbans take shape in the dim cages. Sweat trickles down Rashid's back. He picks up the washcloth and runs it over his neck, puts it under his shirt and wipes his chest, then between his shoulder blades. Without looking at Rashid, Tarik unrolls his towel on the bare floor towards him. Rashid rolls up his own towel and places it around his neck. He squats at the head of his mattress. In the hutches on the other side of the path, the white rectangles hung in front of dark cages make a checker pattern. Three enclosures remain gray, with three oranges lying on the ground inside them. Rashid sits back into the corner like he's watching a show. He wraps his arms around his knees, trying to knead the cramps from his innards. Behind him, between the fence of his cage and the plywood wall, mosquitoes swarm from the sun-singed grass. It's time again.

The loudspeaker crackles. *Allahu akbar! Allahu akbar!—Ash'hadu a 'l-la ilaha illa -'llah. . . .* the wailing. Allah's voice doesn't have any resonance. It winds laboriously up and swirls around the corrugated iron roofs, sinks, recovers, rises again. Tarik tucks the tip of the towel into his makeshift turban. The dish towel makes him into a supplicant. Five times a day he looks like this, as if he knows how life in his cage fits into a grand scheme. *Hayyi 'ala 's-salah! Hayyi 'ala 'l-falah!* Allah sobs, *hayyi 'ala 's-salah, hayyi 'ala 'l-falah.* Five cages closer to Mecca,

Suleyman stands up. Instead of a dish towel, he's wearing a white cap. He slips his sandals off, turns his back to Rashid and steps onto the white towel on the ground. *La ilaha illa -'llah*, the wail, the wail of the camp. They stand at the edge of their towel-sized empires, arms outstretched, palms up as if they wish to catch the song and ladle it into their ears. Allah's wailing song from the loudspeakers of an American prison camp: *Allahu akbar*.

Rashid looks across at the gaps in the prayer row on the other side of the path. Only one of the guys lying down is a non-believer like him. The others are offering a continuous prayer in more extreme fashion: *No food*. It had all begun with a dish towel. Back then Allah still had an American accent. They had taken a prisoner at the far end out of his cage during evening prayers. The MPs ran over the glowing gravel as if somebody had hanged himself. The wiry Afghani interpreter, in a uniform but no hat, came behind them, also running. The shadows slanted in all directions. Even with his face pressed to the fence, Rashid couldn't make out what was happening. He could hear only hoarse snippets of conversation as the prayers rang over the corrugated iron roofs and the oranges across the way—purplish gray under the halogen flood lamps— continued their repetitions. Rashid listened closely, distinguishing the sound of the bolt being opened, the metallic clang of the cage door and the higher-pitched rattling of the chains. Then he watched as a tremor took hold right down the row, cage after cage, a realization that overwhelmed the wailed Arabic commands. One after the other broke off his prayers, left his towel, and pressed against his fence. Rashid only found out what had happened the next day: Instead of his white cap, the prisoner had used a dish towel—and a soldier had ripped it off his head. The unseen prisoner just kept screaming the same sentences over and over again. The words had a dark Pashtun ring to them that reminded Rashid of Mirgul's *Ana*, endlessly mumbling to herself in the damp shack in Peshawar. The recorded voice continued to blare from the speakers, but now other voices were mixed in—he recognized shouts in Urdu and Arabic. As the bound prisoner was whisked by, fists beat on the gates and towels and Korans were waved. Then the loudspeaker cut out and in the silence one of the prisoners shouted *Allahu akbar*. It sounded like a curse.

The first repetition was joined by the entire block. Suddenly they all spoke the same language, the language of Allah. The "ah" of Allah was a curse, a call to arms, a coded slogan. With each chant it grew bigger, louder, higher in pitch, rising above the roofs and swooping back down again. The entire camp echoed with it and became one people. The wire fences shook and shampoo bottles, towels and sandals flew out of the cages. Water and urine splashed onto the path. If the buckets hadn't just been changed, it would have rained shit. Rashid felt incredibly exhilarated. But even so, the more they shouted and raged, the more hemmed in he felt. He pressed his lips together, he growled like an animal, he shook like mad at the bars of the gate and the doorframe. So alone, so narrow, so alone was the moment when all the other prisoners had the same words on their tongues, that he felt he could beat down the walls of his cage under cover of their anger. But the cage was stronger than his despair. When sirens started to sound and the camp was bathed in brighter light from some more distant source, he dropped to his knees, both hands still gripping the chain links, and whimpered.

Finally the loudspeaker went on again. Now it was in English. The voice spoke to *both guards and detainees*, explaining that the camp had been surrounded by Marines and that their orders were to shoot anyone who continued to disturb the peace. Rashid, on the ground, let the nasal speech soothe him; the sound of the announcement took him back to the airplane during his travels, catapulting through the air. And as the announcement was repeated in three more languages, the anger in the camp subsided. But nobody went to sleep. In a quiet, drawn out shadow play, the prayers started over again. Non-stop through the night, MPs patrolled in pairs beneath the flood lights. The tops of their faces were doused in the shadow of the brims of their caps; their mouths, visible beneath, looked grim and worried. In the morning the Muslims refused to pray. The tape of the American reading the text played in vain. At first the chant of *Allahu akbar* from one of the prisoners came faint and distant, but eventually the whole dance started again. Breakfast: *bagels* and eggs pelted down outside the cages. On it went: no midday prayers and no *lunch*. In the afternoon it was announced there would be new cells in the near future, with running water, and that *towels* would be permitted to be used during prayers as long as head coverings could be checked from time to time. The hunger strike crumbled. The ones who continued disappeared at some stage. And from then on the voice over the loudspeaker was an Arabic muezzin.

Rashid stretches out his legs and exhales. His hands drop from his knees to his lap. The orangutans' hands drop to their laps, all the cages speaking in one voice, in one language, a murmured sing-song chorus. *Bismi 'llahi 'r-rahmani 'r-rahim*, the "h" always phlegmy and rasping, and the "i" spiked and high like the tower of a minaret. One hand grips the other as if it were someone else's, holding it upright—and the effect is that of a wrestling ring or a bar brawl. Nobody's head is down. With the turbans they've grown as tall as the green and brown-clad MPs in their military caps. The soldiers stand in the compound, out in the fields, in toadstool-colored uniforms, in a strict military line, ready to storm the stalls and march people away in the right direction, *ihdina 's-sirata 'l-mustaqim*, straight to the east, *Amin*.

Rashid knows the music and all the choreographed moves of this ballet. There's no suspense. He waits, but he doesn't expect anything new. *Allahu akbar* again and again. They bend forward, they genuflect, they believe. In what? The only thing in the direction they are bowing is the enemy. It's where the watchtower is. It's where the sun comes up. Every day the same thing, every day a little earlier. And every day begins with the short morning prayers in the half-light of dawn. The sun comes up and the loudspeaker goes on. America regiments itself by the sun, and Allah marches to America's drum. All the prisoners march with him, their knees on the camp's towels. They put their hands down on either side, right and left, touch their foreheads to these damn cage floors: *subhana rabbiya 'l-a'la* again and again. Every time their skulls hit the floor it sends a shiver through Rashid, twitching through his whole body, more than any boot stomps. Maybe it's the multiplication effect that gives all this wretched bowing a defiant pride. They all see in each other their own reflection, screened across countless wire squares. One person praying is nobody; many praying can do much more. Sometimes when he meets another prisoner on the path—six of them altogether, two prisoners and a soldier on each side of each prisoner—he sees the symbol on the bowed forehead. The bluish gray spot doesn't look as if it's been caused by the ground; it looks as if it's been put there by a powerful force, someone like Allah.

Someone who knows why they are here. Someone who follows them and lets them know what they need to do. *Allahu akbar.* They all rise as one, rear ends on their heels, hands on their knees. *Subhana rabbiya 'l-a'la! Allahu akbar.* They all stand and start again from the beginning.

The sun is already glinting on the coils of razor wire atop the buildings. Beneath them the prisoners' outfits glow, marionettes in orange costumes lifted up and then thrown down again. Their shadows dance across the path. Rashid sees himself in the audience of the puppet theater, his own rear end on his heels and his hands on his knees. He's sweating and his lower body is cramping. The mosquitoes whir. It never stops. Day and night, in every light, in every waking second, it can hit him and drag him back—back to the point before which he can't remember anything. Deaf, blind and unable to move, stuck rehashing the beginning of it all. Each time he tries to get back to before his arrival here, searching for a way out. But the nightmare just plays out the same way all over again, and he lands on his knees exactly like the men in front of him, again and again. This is his own version of prayer. Most of the time it begins in the guest house in Katmandu with Mirgul. Sometimes just before that, during his hike in the mountains. Sometimes elsewhere during his trip, in Amritsar or Lahore. Often it begins only in Peshawar. And sometimes all the way back in Delhi or even in Hamburg. Blind, with a hood over his head, his memory stakes him to some mile marker and leaves him tethered there. He looks around, sees his own trail. The steps always head in the pre-ordained direction of the prison camp. The closer he gets to the camp, the more panicked his search for other paths becomes. He stops and pushes and looks for a detour. Sometimes he succeeds in veering off and striking out in a direction where there is no trail at all, no ground, a false path. What if. What if he'd been able to hit a bend and just keep gliding, like a ski jumper continuing his arc in the air. Maybe he gets sick back in Hamburg, real sick, wastes away all through February. Maybe the airplane needs repairs or his *Nani* dies. He'll never meet her. It makes him sad. But everything's fine. Maybe he falls during the climb and when they find him the Nepalese take him to recover someplace far away from the *Tibet Guest House*. He loses Mirgul in Amritsar and heads to Goa with a group of backpackers. He loses Mirgul in Lahore. He never meets Mirgul in Katmandu. He turns down his invitation, isn't interested in an Afghani refugee family living on the border. He doesn't want to go. Doesn't want to go. He sticks around and finds a better, more colorful destination on Flick street. He never goes out into the street in Peshawar. Not without his passport. He decides to stay with the *Ana* and help her pack, waiting at the shack until it's time to go to Jalalabad. He daydreams. But he always ends up on the ground, in a basement, in a truck, on an airplane, unable to get out. *Hands up, don't move.* He's surrounded by red, surrounded by darkness, on his knees. Everything in stages. A journey to nothingness, all the while on his knees. And whenever he opens his eyes he finds himself in another dream, a tougher, stickier dream of fear from which he never wakes up. Always the same, here, now. It never ends.

They drop to all fours again. Suleyman's rear end lifts up off his heels. Tarik's rear towers above his head. Rashid's innards surge upwards, too, like they know the rhythm of the prayers. The food works its way through his body, as inexorably as Allah's appearances. From dawn to dusk. From wolfing it down to crapping it out. Prayers end with you kneeling; food with you squatting. And whether you are on the ground or on a bucket, you put your hands on your knees in a show of resignation, of monotony, of having digested it all. *A 't-tahiyatu li 'llah.* But you don't have to. You can just lay there and let everything pass you by, like the oranges on the mattresses. They don't pray and they don't eat. Rashid begrudges them their apathy. They don't move, nothing moves them, and at some point they won't even breathe anymore. He's often tried to emulate them. He stretches out on his mattress and waits for the waiting to stop. Sometimes the monotony fades away. The sounds flow together, the surroundings press into his skin. Hot, contaminated air laps at his body like an oily liquid slowly carrying him away. His consciousness also becomes liquid and trickles through the fence, seeps through the camp, feeling at home. He doesn't feel foreign and doesn't arouse any suspicion when he roams around, trickles through the chain links and camouflage netting and coils of razor wire, around the poles holding the halogen flood lamps and the wooden posts holding up raised buildings, past the watchtowers and barracks and along boundary walls. Never further afield. As long as he can keep himself in this state, there is no outside. When he ignores the things keeping him in, he also forgets the things beyond—mountains, the ocean.

Just as his dreams roust him, so too does his body. Continuous stomach sickness, trouble breathing, dizziness, sweating, itching and the beat of his heart all hinder his efforts to clear his mind, to forget. Finally the hunger brings him back. Actually, it's not hunger. It's the generic desire for generic slop. It's a dull feeling in his brain and on his tongue. Whenever he finishes shoveling one of the airplane meals in using a *spork* and his fingers, he hopes he'll never have to eat again. Every bite makes him even more of a prisoner: on the outside the orange outfit, and on inside his guts stuffed with the taste of the camp. He longs for emptiness. He longs to feel genuine ravenousness. But then they bring a plastic tray and his longing collapses. Rashid cowers in the corner, ever more ashamed. The embarrassing compulsion to eat always ends up in the waste bucket. *A 's-salamu alaykum wa rahmatu 'llah*. Prayers are over. Heads swivel to the left and to the right, *a 's-salamu alaykum*. The hunger strikers don't stir.

Turbans disappear from heads, and towels from the ground. Rashid stands up. He picks up the dishtowel from the edge of the waste bucket and hangs it on the back wall of his cage. He dips a washcloth in the lukewarm water of the other bucket and hangs it right next to the dishtowel. He wraps the blanket around his waist and undoes the buttons of his pants. He pulls the waste bucket out from the corner a little and sits down on it with his back to the row of cages on the opposite side of the path, and partly turned away from Tarik. His tent-shaped form is cast on the plywood wall, set amid the crosshatched shadows of the fencing. He holds the twisted tip of the blanket in his fists, holding it under his chin. He rests his elbows on his knees. He's careful not to let the overhanging blanket knock over the things piled nearby. He's got the shampoo bottle, the liquid soap, the *mint flavor* toothpaste and his toothbrush sitting on top of the Koran. To appease Tarik, he keeps the white prayer cap spread out beneath the book. Tarik couldn't stand to see it sitting on the ground. The first one he had had Indian letters inside. *Father Indian Muslim, mother German protestant* they had written down after initially questioning him. They had assumed he was an Urdu-speaking Muslim. He had been pleased about the book. But then it had been impossible for him to suffer the view of the characters, which he had studied as a kid in his father's old magazines, trying to figure out which kind of secret objects were tangled up in the rows of clotheslines. A few days later a soldier came by his cage and introduced himself as a *Muslim chaplain*. He was the only soldier who ever introduced himself by name and his was Islam, of all things. He asked about Rashid's faith. Just to be able to talk to him Rashid said *Muslim* and was given an English version of the Koran. But Rashid's broken English had left Islam-MP uneasy, and later he came back and proudly presented Rashid with a German version. *The holy book in your mother-tongue.* Rashid would gladly have kept both books, but he had to give back the English version. You only got one Koran. *Those who reject Our Signs, We shall soon cast into the Fire; As often as their skins are roasted through, We shall change them for fresh skins, that they may taste The Penalty: for Allah is Exalted in Power, Wise.* The suras swirled around his head like the mosquitoes. *But those who believe and do deeds of righteousness, We shall soon admit to Gardens, with rivers flowing beneath— their eternal home; Therein shall they have Companions pure and holy: We shall admit them to shades, cool and ever deepening.*

  The rim of the bucket presses sharply into his thighs and buttocks. He pulls his feet alongside and tries to shift his weight. At the outhouse he has to sit all the way down because of all the weight he's carrying. The hardest part is maneuvering his pants down past the belt securing his leg irons. His cuffed wrists sit in his naked lap while he sits. Between the cloying heat, the mist of the disinfectant they spray the stalls with after each use, and the dizziness he feels from emptying himself, he almost passes out. But he still prefers to go in those stalls because, with their trap doors, he can at least leave the shit behind. He doesn't like to have it nearby. He doesn't want to be alone with it. It smells of sickness. It smells of fear. It reminds him of the children's hospital in Mainz where he'd had to roll the IV stand to the bathroom with him. He had started crying over the toilet bowl there. The yellowish stuff inside it had a disgusting, artificial smell. It was worse than the raw ache in his stomach and worse than his homesickness. Rashid doesn't even know how he smells anymore. He leans over and picks up the bottle of liquid soap. He puts a few drops on the washcloth and wipes himself clean. He holds his breath and stands up, covers the bucket with the dishtowel and shoves it back into the corner. Securing the blanket in his armpits he hikes up his orange pants and then throws the blanket back onto the mattress. He pours water over the washcloth once, twice, wrings it out on the floor and then uses one of his sandals to squeegee the puddle of water out of his cage. He pours water over his hands and scrubs them. He stands in front of the door, reaches up almost to the roof and hooks his fingers into the chain link. Just outside, the wet spot on the dusty white gravel is already fading.

The shadows have lengthened. They recede in the morning, disappear at noontime and then lengthen all afternoon. Right before and after the pause at noon, when the contours are at their harshest, you can see the direction shift. The edges of the roofs on the cages on the other side of the path are a good place on which to see the shadows change direction. So are the blades of grass on either side of the door and behind the back wall of the cage. You can also watch the shadows shift in an indentation or on stone. The pattern the shadows make on the ground moves like a viscous puddle. They move in silent increments like a clock hand, and like a clock hand they seem not to move at all if you're looking right at them. Shadows move more slowly than minutes. But whenever he doubts they are in fact moving, he can just track that change from light to dark and watch them creeping forth. Now they flow into one another and blur. The world is motionless, like at night under the stare of artificial lights. If anything's still moving, it's hidden from view. Something knocks hollowly: short-short-short-long, short-short-short-long. Sometimes faint, trailing off, sometimes louder. Once in a while there's a pop, like wood against wood, between lengthy pauses. They're building to the north. It sounds as if heavy things are being dropped in place. Distant rumbling. Metal hinges squeak, engines idle and rev. It's calm among the cages. Somewhere out of view a bucket scrapes against the ground. There's nobody on the path. Soon they'll come to take prisoners to *recreation time,* two or three pairs of MPs shuttling them in *three-pieces* back and forth past wire fences, tarps and camouflage netting. They take them to a small, enclosed concrete square where a lone dirty, white soccer ball sits. A couple of kicks, their rubber sandals on leather, twice a week. The view from the square is of light-colored wooden buildings, watchtowers, and the low interrogators' barracks with air conditioning units in the windows, and, high above the coiled razor wire on top, the flag—stars and happy stripes. Afterwards they go to the showers, each one as big as their cages. The stalls reek of fresh paint. The walls are white; the wire mesh roof and door are painted green. A push on the button and a stream of lukewarm water comes down from the showerhead mounted high up on the wall. The MPs—never women—wait outside watching, with the restraints in their hands. They reattach them through two sets of holes in the door, one at hip height and one at floor level. Naked twice a week, twice a week the feel of soap rubbing across your skin, and the cooling effect of water evaporating from your body. But not today. Today Rashid only gets to watch others come and go. Along with the MP escorts comes the doctor—*need any help?* Once in a while Islam the *chaplain* comes by, too. Then dinner. Evening prayers. Twilight, the flood lights, nighttime. Time is supposed to pass with the shadows. Not here.

Rashid has never seen the wall beyond which the world lies. On the way to the soccer field there are points where he can see past the razor wire and catch a glimpse of a monotonous landscape of scrub-brush covered hillocks. But he hardly ever has a chance to glance at it: *head down*. The soldiers' houses must be somewhere beyond that. And even further away are streets, cities, a big island and open ocean all around it—an ocean behind walls. Sometimes Rashid tries to escape the present by getting a view of the world surrounding the cages. To do that, he has to go back—back to where he arrived here, where the airplane landed. Back to that deep blue afternoon, with the deafening roar, the droning and screeching, the hum of tanks and the whoosh of helicopter blades. Rashid closes his eyes and slowly twists himself upwards, boring his way through the corrugated iron roof, until he stands free atop an invisible spindle. His feet aim down at his cage even though from this height he can't tell which one is his. The wider his field of view becomes, the smaller the world holding him seems, and as it shrinks so does the shadowy mess he's stuck in, shrinking into crates and trails, booths at a fair, carrying cases for pets, ground cover. Everything disconnects and uncoils, rolling down to the ocean. The scrub-brush—now formed of barracks and razor wire—becomes ever more impenetrable, and the surface of blue light—the bright glassy ocean—recedes ever further. Sometimes the water gleams right in front of his eyes, before he has covered the distance into the sky, and lures him into lunging recklessly through the razor-wire scrub-brush. That's why Rashid is careful spending his time this way. He has to painstakingly make his way up a few feet at a time and let the pressure equalize—otherwise he'll crash and his daydream will smash on the concrete floor of his cage. Imagining gazing at himself from above is his last resort. He reserves this for the worst times, the times when there's no other way to avoid asking questions about the future. But to ask those questions is even more dangerous. The doctor doesn't answer. The *chaplain* doesn't answer. And the silence hurts more than any answer.

There's a soft clang off to the right. Tarik is crouching on the ground fiddling with the bottom of the fence. He has somehow succeeded in picking a long blade of grass. Now he's sticking it out of the fence wire. Rashid lowers himself to his knees between the mattress and the water bucket and leans over toward the fence facing Tarik's cage. Tarik nods his head and puts his finger to his lips for Rashid to be quiet. *Animal,* he whispers. *Animal very bad.* He forms his left hand into a claw. Rashid stares at the sparse turf between their cages. The sand colored dirt beneath the partly green, partly burnt grass is mottled with tiny splotches of sunlight. *Look,* Tarik says. He uses the long blade he's holding as a pointer. Rashid puts his forehead to the fence. There are hairline cracks in the dry dirt. Crumbs of soil and pebbles of gravel gather at the base of the clumps of grass. *Look,* Tarik says again. *Move quick.* He pokes. A lump of dry dirt rolls in Rashid's direction and something shoots twitching and jerking through the grass at a right angle to the trajectory of the lump of dirt. For a second Rashid sees an earth-colored form shooting toward the path; it comes to a stop level with the front of the cage. Tarik scrambles into the corner of his cage. Rashid cautiously moves the water bucket to the side and cowers in his own corner. An arm's length from the cage fence is a bizarre fist-size bump on the ground. It looks like an articulated root from which thin flexible appendages stick out, two of which are arched like frog legs. The legs are arranged around a shiny, hairy finger encased in a dark segmented shell with a nut-sized bulb at one end. The thing just sits there. The legs cast long, wispy shadows. *Spider*, says Rashid. Tarik shakes his head. *No spider*. He holds up both hands and spreads his fingers. *Ten arms*, he says. *Bad animal*, he says, and sticks two fingers into his arm like fangs. Then he reaches behind him and pulls out his military water flask. He unscrews the top and holds it up high. *Shower*, he says, grinning. He squeezes the flask and water arches out of his cage and splatters to the ground. Rashid hears the patter of water and sees that the animal isn't there anymore. But he picks up the jerking motion again, and it's heading straight for him. A grinding noise accompanies the motion and he flinches backwards as the thing brushes against his feet. He looks down and sees the beast shoot past his mattress, its nut-like head leading the way like a battering ram and feelers wagging between swirling legs. Two of the legs stick out at right angles to its body like pennants waving as it scoots across the concrete floor. It runs into the waste bucket, the last legs round the bucket, and it heads out the back. Rashid, pressed into the corner looking over his shoulder, can still see it in his mind tracing the diagonal path across the cage floor. He looks back at the spot where the water is oozing into the ground like a shadow within a shadow. He can feel his heart pumping hard.

Tarik is still smiling. *Move quick*, he says again, screwing the top back on the flask. Rashid walks over and puts the water bucket back in place. Behind him he hears steps coming. They pause. Chains rattle. The first orders to exit reverberate in the air. Rashid lays down on his mattress and folds his hands behind his head. They're moist. MPs tromp past in pairs. Across the way one of the oranges is already standing with his back to his gate. Rashid closes his eyes. He senses the heat flagging. A breeze caresses the bottom of his feet. The familiar racket swirls more quietly around him. Crunching boots, shuffling, metallic clanging, the routine commands, the almost soft *get your head down, come on, go ahead.* The construction has subsided and all that's left is the distant pounding—short-short-short-long, short-short-short-long—giving the other gentle sounds a rhythm. He thinks of the sound of the water splattering to the ground again, and it reminds him of the water from the shower splashing in the stall—he can almost feel the cool, wet shower floor beneath his feet. His hands glide under his arms, scrub, run down his sides. Suds form on his chest and ooze down to his pubic hair. His knees twitch as if he's just been jolted by a minor electric shock. There's a short holdup, then it trickles down his skin again, loosening and stretching his body, it grows, he bumps against the wall. A shadow darts past his feet. He can't move. Outside they're shouting, pounding on the shower door. But then Tarik appears. *No shower*, he cries out, *no go today.* Rashid sits up, his cock tenses. He's sweating. His shirt sticks to his back.

Tarik's face is up against the fence now, pressing so hard against the chain-links that the skin of his cheeks looks quilted. His mouth is scrunched to the side. MPs keep him in place, one holding up his arms while another chains his ankles together. At the door to his cage stands a female soldier. Tarik's cage looks empty. The sheets are in a pile on the mattress and the water flask and Koran are on the floor. Both buckets are sitting out front, next to the open cage door. The two men peel Tarik off the fence. They shove his arms in front of him, cuff him, and snap the cuffs to the belt. *No go*, he screams. *You pigs, fucking pigs.* The blond MP grabs the hair on the back of Tarik's neck, pulling his head back. Just as he lets go, the other one, the smaller one, shoves him out the door. Tarik's forehead slams into the crossbeam. His knees buckle and he starts to lose his footing, but the smaller MP holds him up by the belt. He slumps forward. The blond MP leans forward, grabs him by the hair again, and jerks him upright. He puts his face right up to Tarik's: *You talk too much*, he says. He lets go of his head, steps around him and out of the cage, glancing over at Rashid. Tarik lurches toward the back of the cage but then the smaller MP manages to position himself so he can get enough leverage to shove him out of the cage. The blond MP catches him just outside. Tarik's feet drag loudly between the boot steps of the two MPs as they yank him away. A dog barks wildly. Rashid is still sitting upright on his mattress. Rashid watches as the woman enters Tarik's cage and bundles up the Koran with the sheets and towels. She's wearing rubber gloves. It's *Call-me-MP*.

Rashid watches as she walks off in the other direction, a bucket in each hand and the bundle tucked under one arm. It's a nice image: the female shape in a uniform and the two white cylinders dangling on each side like a scale. He pictures her wearing the balled up sheets and towels as a huge turban. But then she nods at another soldier, unable to lift an arm to salute, and nearly drops the would-be turban. She walks out of sight as the doctor approaches, passing quickly by the empty cages. Without breaking stride he points at Rashid as he goes by and says, *Everything OK?* Then he's gone.

The dog won't stop barking. The sky is grayish blue, and the last of the direct light is fading. A few last rays of sun fall between the cages. The darkest time of the day is fast approaching. Rashid looks at Tarik's empty cage, the door left standing open. Once they turn on the flood lights he might be able to pick out the blade of grass Tarik had used to prod the giant ten-legged spider. As they switch out the buckets after evening prayers, they'll spray Tarik's cage with disinfectant. Rashid has learned from Tarik that evening prayers must take place after sunset, and that night prayers take place even later, after the twilight has completely faded and it's dark. He thinks back to the evening of his first day here, the fear he felt when the flood lights came on, and the childish sobs that welled up in him when the lights stayed on even after night prayers. He had squatted at the door to his cage and looked across at the oranges elsewhere bedding down on their mattresses. Since then he too had learned to curl up and sleep under the false light. The cold light and warm humidity lulls him into an artificial half-sleep, sleeping under electricity. Sometimes he hears the patrols go marching by, dogs barking, the static and crackle of walkie-talkies. But what really gets to him are the things nearby, things that sleep during the day and are attracted by the artificial light just like the bugs that swarm around the flood lights: invisible critters in the grass, moths whose fat bodies plunk against the corrugated iron, flying beetles that fall to the floor. And the never-ending buzz of mosquitoes. Some of the prisoners spread towels over their faces at night, but Rashid always feels the need to be able to see and breathe. He puts his feet under the covers and sometimes scrunches the sheet around his ears. He usually sleeps on his left side. He can see his own shadow on the cold neon white of his sheets. His outfit looks purple under the flood lights and the blue blanket gray. The floor is black and the buckets glow like two cylindrical lamps in the corners. These are freakish colors, the colors of nightmares. He tries to keep his back to them, pressing his face so close to the fence that he can't even see it. He looks out across the bluish grass at the next cage. The form curled up in it offers the calming effect of a mirror image.

Tarik is gone. The sand-colored spider is gone. Rashid is afraid of the night. He looks toward the watch tower, through the empty cages, and sees Suleyman pacing back and forth in his cage. Two steps one way, two steps back the other. His throat is tight. The waste bucket stinks. He can hear the chuckwagon working its way down the rows, still quite soft, still out of view. Soon he'll stand, they'll chain him to the fence, open the cage, put the food on the floor, lock up the cage again and, from outside, unchain him and pull the restraints back out through the chain link. He won't bite their hands or threaten them. He won't curse at them or throw the shit in his waste bucket at them. He wants to eat: rice, red beans, cabbage, a banana—just like yesterday and the day before that. He sits in the southeast corner of his cage, stretches out his legs, leans back, and closes his eyes. He opens his right eye, then his left. In the distance he can hear cage doors opening and chains rattling. Bluish light, reddish light. Blue, red. The world switches back and forth as he opens and shuts each eye. Concrete, steel beams, chain diamonds, blades of grass and one last ray of sunlight angled across the ground, no wider than the spine of his Koran. Blue, red. Then a flash just above the ground. A colorful flap tumbles through the beam of sunlight, opening and closing. It flutters into the shadows, a black and white eye on each wingtip and a red dot at the bottom of each wing. He follows it with his eyes to the plywood wall, flitting just above the ground. It turns and flutters off along the wall. Without taking his eyes off it, he slides on his knees across the mattress and presses himself into the corner, staring after it. The pair of red dots flit on his retinas long after they're out of sight.

III. *Kill.* Reward and Reaction

Yes, my name is Rashid Bakhrani. I don't know Urdu beyond a couple of words—*Baba, Nani, adab, bacha, habib, chai, shukria.* I don't speak Arabic either, but I know the prayer, *Allahu akbar, ash'hadu a 'l-la ilaha illa -'llah.* The only two words I know in Pashtun are *wror* and *Ana.* I can't speak any Dari at all. My English is OK—I took it for six years in school. I went to school in Hamburg. I was born in Mainz. In *Deutschland.* Germany. I read the Koran in German: O Ye who believe! Fear Allah as He should be feared, and die not except in a state of Islam. And so on. I've completely forgotten what German sounds like. Yes, I'm German. And Muslim, yes. My father's Muslim. He was born Muslim and never converted. No, he's not German—but he is a German citizen. He's Indian. I don't know—maybe I'm not even Muslim. No, I don't know why I'm here. I was on vacation. It was my first time in India. I was visiting my grandmother. I dreamt the other day that she had died. Yes, she's Muslim. No, she doesn't speak German, and hardly any English. But we were able to communicate anyway. No, I don't speak Urdu.

They had come for him in the morning, without warning. He didn't know where they were taking him or why. It was still dark, and he'd finally fallen asleep, tossing and turning, dreaming—and when they took him outside he was shaky on his feet. At first it was the usual: gravel crunching beneath boots and shouts of *head down.* But then the sound of the boots changed as they crossed a wide, paved yard crisscrossed by shadows; a row of stakes, then stone steps, *lift your feet*, a set of green double doors, white tarps, thick bulletproof-glass walls, a soundproof hallway, chills, a steel door, fluorescent lighting, a wall. Then it was as if they were pressing him into the depths of the wall itself. Beyond it was the nothingness he had already come to know. First his face—black-out goggles, ear plugs, a face mask—then his hands, into thick gloves. The fear hit him just as hard as the first time he'd gone through this. The only thing supporting him was their hands, clenched to his upper arms like a vice. On he went, lurching, staggering, further into this tunnel of darkness, of silence, where all he could hear were his own gasps for air. The vice-grip on his arms, the floor beneath his feet— that was it. Each step forward was tentative, a stumble. Then they let go of him. He stood alone in the dark, with no hands, no ears, for ages. He tried to keep his balance. He worried he was on a ledge, surrounded by an abyss. He stood with his feet much too close to one another. He waited and tried not to think about falling. His legs were shaking, but he dared not lower himself to the ground or drop to his knees. At some moments he was possessed with the crazy idea this might be the first stop on his return voyage—that this might be the beginning of the end of his imprisonment. His body wasn't in pain. Except that his head hurt from the suction of the goggles on his eyes and the cups on his ears. In order not to work himself into a panic, he tried to keep his hands still. The hard metal around his wrists helped with that. He could picture the cuffs in his mind; they were familiar. The first time he'd had them on it felt as if the skin on his two forearms had fused together. That his wrists had actually been wrapped in duct tape he only realized when they tore it off.

He waited. He longed for the strong arms of the MPs, their orders, their pokes and prods. He wanted to go back to his cage. Just as he began tentatively to shuffle his chained feet a few inches forward, they were back. They guided him a few paces across the smooth, springy floor, took off his gloves, and brought him out of the mute blackness into a light so bright he was as blind as he'd been in the dark. Red seeped through his eyelids and cut the glare each time he blinked. Through the whiteout came voices, lots of voices, lots of languages, lots of questions, quickly, one after another. It reeked of sweat and uniforms, but also of something oddly clean—toothpaste, aftershave, or even cologne. He realized this was it, the interrogation; he'd finally made it. A wild, panicked wave of happiness washed over him and his legs began to shake again even as he reminded himself that he wasn't supposed to move, that he needed to keep it together at all costs, that he needed to concentrate—just like at school, during the hardest exam—to listen hard, think, and answer, to answer precisely, correctly.

I don't have any Arab friends in Hamburg, or any Pakistani friends, or Afghani. I don't know any college students. Yes, I'm 20, but I'm not going to college. I work in my father's shop. Yes, he's Muslim. No, I'm not Muslim. I never pray. Neither does my father. My father doesn't have any Arab friends, or Pakistanis—except maybe relatives. It's possible some of his relatives live in Pakistan, but I only know of the ones in India. Yes, it's true I'm circumcised. That was done when I was a baby, in Mainz. My father wanted it done—maybe because of his family. He's got relatives in Germany and India.

They know everything. Their questions come out of the light, one after another, quickly, in different voices. They emerge from different parts of the room—none of

58

which he can see—first in English, then in German. He hangs his head and peers down at his feet; his toes, in rubber sandals, seem far away. Once a question has been repeated in German, he has to say something. And he has to stand, stand still, though his body is twitching and trembling and his instinct is to run. He's scared. He isn't scared of the other people, because they can't do anything wrong. They're just watching and listening to him, and observing what they see and hear. That's what scares him. He can't trust his legs, and his own voice sounds strange to him—it doesn't suit the situation, it's too weak, too ordinary. His German sounds naïve and awkward. Whatever he says is repeated quietly in English, like a secret. Then there's a pause. He never has a chance to think. He has to try to hold on to the words and figure out what is happening to them. The words disappear into the unseen space and transform themselves. He worries about them—about the words he says—and about the possibility that they will come back to him altered, changed into something else, something dangerous.

Yes, I was in Delhi. My grandmother lives there. I went there because she's old, because my grandfather had died, because I had inherited some money—money for a store, my own store. No, it was my first trip to India. I got a visa for Pakistan, too. I had never been to Pakistan and I had never been to Afghanistan. I hadn't intended to go to Afghanistan, but I got invited there. No, I didn't want to fight. I just wanted to travel. I didn't want to fight. The war was already over. I don't know. I only know one name, Mirgul. I don't know his last name. There was also a grandmother. I mean, another grandmother. No, I don't know anybody else there. Yes, they were Muslims. No, they weren't Taliban. Yes, there were men around. Maybe they were Taliban. Yes, some men were there. But they came there only to sleep.

The English voice begins to shout. Rashid can't understand, but now he can make out a man with a big head, his arm slashing up and down as he shouts. He's in a uniform—not everyone wears one—maybe an officer's uniform. He's sitting up front, slamming his fist on the table. Rashid can't concentrate. The German voice is too soft, and difficult to understand anyway, with a heavy American accent. Now the German voice goes silent and the officer shouts on. Rashid's whole body is wet. The light is hot. And he's afraid he's going to piss himself. Then it's quiet. Rashid waits. He isn't being asked questions. He can't ask questions. He has to go to the bathroom. He can't reach his crotch. He presses his knees together. He begins to sway. He needs to prop himself up and starts to move backwards, taking tiny steps, slowly, toward where he assumes a wall must be. The officer jumps up. *Don't move*, he screams, and then quieter, grumbling, *let's go*. It hits him in the lower back, a pair of sharp blows, two fists at once, to the right and left of his spinal column. He doubles over. Then one in the gut, right below his ribs. He reels backwards, the face in front of his broad and red, a familiar face: It's one of his two MPs. They're still with him. Rashid gasps, twists and coughs; he doesn't have to go to the bathroom anymore. He stays on his feet. He squints out at the light and tries to see the faces of the observers. Too bright. Another voice says, *Mr. Bakhrani, tell us the story of your time in Peshawar.* This is repeated in German.

Again silence. Rashid closes his eyes. Waiting in the shack on the outskirts of town was dreary, but he had friends in the city. He went into town every day with Mirgul—or without. Horns blaring, bikes everywhere, they were Taliban. Yes, some men were there. But they came there only to sleep.

The English voice begins to shout. Rashid can't understand, but now he can make out a man with a big head, his arm slashing up and down as he shouts. He's in a uniform—not everyone wears one—maybe an officer's uniform. He's sitting up front, slamming his fist on the table. Rashid can't concentrate. The German voice is too soft, and difficult to understand anyway, with a heavy American accent. Now the German voice goes silent and the officer shouts on. Rashid's whole body is wet. The light is hot. And he's afraid he's going to piss himself. Then it's quiet. Rashid waits. He isn't being asked questions. He can't ask questions. He has to go to the bathroom. He can't reach his crotch. He presses his knees together. He begins to sway. He needs to prop himself up and starts to move backwards, taking tiny steps, slowly, toward where he assumes a wall must be. The officer jumps up. *Don't move*, he screams, and then quieter, grumbling, *let's go*. It hits him in the lower back, a pair of sharp blows, two fists at once, to the right and left of his spinal column. He doubles over. Then one in the gut, right below his ribs. He reels backwards, the face in front of his broad and red, a familiar face: It's one of his two MPs. They're still with him. Rashid gasps, twists and coughs; he doesn't have to go to the bathroom anymore. He stays on his feet. He squints out at the light and tries to see the faces of the observers. Too bright. Another voice says, *Mr. Bakhrani, tell us the story of your time in Peshawar.* This is repeated in German.

Again silence. Rashid closes his eyes. Waiting in the shack on the outskirts of town was dreary, but he had friends in the city. He went into town every day with Mirgul—or without. Horns blaring, bikes everywhere,

people selling things. He had helped fix the pickup truck
in the backyard. There were goats in the garage. When
they took breaks he would sit with the others in the barber shop out front, laugh, drink tea, get a shave. Then
came the rain and the riot. They all went out into the
street, lots of men, they pumped their fists in the air, he
raised his fist, screams and choruses, *Allahu akbar, jihad,
marg bar Amrika.* Police sirens. The women disappeared
from the sides of the street. The men from the barber shop
were gone. Rocks flew through the air and landed in the
mud around him. All of a sudden police in brown uniforms were everywhere. He was cudgeled. He fell to the
ground. He lifted his head. Boots. He couldn't wipe his
face or stand up. They were holding him down. They put
handcuffs on him, marched him away and stuck him in a
basement. Then came the Americans, the ride in a truck
with a bag over his head, the airplane. *Would you, please,*
from a deep voice, gently.

It was Mirgul's family, children, the *Ana*—the
grandmother—and his aunt. They all lived in a shack,
refugees. They wanted to get back to Afghanistan. They
weren't against America. Yes, some of the men may have
fought in the war. One was dead, Mirgul's uncle—but not
his father. His father was in Jalalabad. I was supposed to
meet him. They were nice, all waiting on the truck. The
grandmother was packing things up, I went with Mirgul.
He knew people in the city, in Peshawar. Yes, Afghanis,
men, yes. A few of them spoke English. They all wanted to
get back home. I wanted to go with them at first, but then
I thought I'd rather go to Goa, on the ocean, in the sun. It
was cold in Peshawar, damp and muddy. I have no idea
whether they were Taliban. No, I didn't know them, not
before then. Al Qaida, no, I don't know anything about Al
Qaida. I didn't understand much of what was said. Yes,

Urdu, and Pashtun probably, and English. No Dari. I don't know—I can't speak Dari. Yes, it was a demonstration. I wasn't attending the demonstration, I just happened to be there. I'm not anti-America. No, I don't want to kill Americans.

He had assumed it would be easier. He isn't prepared. He has lost track of time in his cage. Too much time, too little, too much—he doesn't know. What happened before then seems so far away. He doesn't want to look back. He doesn't want to look forward, either. Now he has to come up with a story. Last night is keeping him from thinking straight. It was a bad night, the night after his trip to the infirmary, a night full of noise and enemies, lots of images and little sleep. When during morning prayers the floodlights were turned off, he wasn't sure what he had dreamed and what had been real. The trip to the infirmary was real—that's where it all began. He knew the long, gleaming, white hallways with their fluorescent lights everywhere and the gangway with the green swinging doors. He knew the examination room from the time he had been strapped into a military stretcher for days with his swollen eye, hot and throbbing. Maybe it had been a mosquito bite. It was also there he had gotten his first shot. But he didn't need this latest shot—he wasn't sick. The doctor seemed older than before, and the pale, round face beneath his shiny forehead looked harder than when he walked through the yard between the cages. *It's an order*, he said, and he said that if he had to, he would call in plenty of people to hold Rashid down. The MPs waiting by the door came in immediately and Rashid said *okay*. They kicked him in the back of the knees anyway, shoved him onto the gurney, and while one held his shoulders, the other lowered his pants and tied him down. They rolled him back to his cell on the gurney even though he could have walked. He wasn't sick. Though now his chest and throat were tightening. Dinner also tasted different than usual, and he sweated as he struggled to get the rice and chickpeas past the lump in his throat. Later he had chills and his stomach was uneasy. Under the blanket, which he had pulled up to his neck, he passed gas more disgusting than anything that had ever before come out of him. But despite that, he eventually pulled the blanket up over his head as well—his fits of shivering made the noises, voices and music in the floodlit yard sound like a radio stuck on the seek function. Some of the voices had faces that looked down on him from outside the cage walls, some even had bodies. They leaned down and threatened him—they would kick him they said, or strangle or crush him. They shook the gate, beat on the chain-link walls and barked: *In your face, wake up, punk, you'll shit bullets, good morning bugfucker, terrorists never sleep, we'll lay you out.* They patrolled with dogs. Rashid didn't understand it all, but he did know they weren't going to leave him in peace. When the wake-up patrol started its round he still had the blanket over his head. It was the stocky Uzbek in the next cage who rousted him. He wanted to talk to the soldiers. He cursed in his inscrutable language, punched the wire fencing and made gestures to Rashid that made it clear he, too, had been unable to sleep. It had not been a dream.

This is no dream, either. Not the bright lights, not the voices. They keep repeating, overlapping each other. He can understand a lot, but the interpreter is keeping him from thinking. He can't concentrate. He can barely stand. He's tired. He starts from the beginning. I wanted to visit my homeland. I'm Muslim. I'm Indian. Gandhi was a great man. He vanquished the English. He wasn't Muslim, but he wasn't against them, either. I didn't feel like going home. Everybody said the war was over and I thought the Americans had left. I wanted to see what it was like after a war. There were Americans in Germany, too. I saw them—they came to Carnival in Mainz. They dropped bombs, against the Nazis. I don't support Nazis and I don't support the Taliban, but I don't support the Americans and I don't support war. If there was a war, I'd fight. I'd protect myself and my family, my grandmother, Mirgul's grandmother. Men have to fight. No, I wasn't training in Peshawar. I just sat around with the guys, as friends, drank tea, and helped them with their truck. Yes, I wanted to cross the border with them, go to Jalalabad, yes, and maybe on to Kabul. I thought Kabul might not be bad, and some of the people in Peshawar wanted to go there. I might have ridden with them. Yes, the vehicle was already there, it just needed to be repaired. It was an old flatbed truck. It could have carried a lot of people. No, there were no weapons. I suppose there could have been some stowed in the garage, but I never saw any.

The officer starts shouting again. *Don't tell us fairytales.* His fist crashes down on the desk. Rashid opens his eyes. Nobody hits him. He stares at the floor. He hears a new voice, slower, more nasal. *Listen*, the new voice says, *I'll tell you what happened*, and the interpreter follows in German. You went to Delhi and then up to Katmandu, where you made contact with Mirgul. Mirgul Shinwari. That's his name. The two of you flew back to Delhi—you paid for his ticket—and then you went to Peshawar. It's tough to get there. You needed him as a guide. You needed the family in Kharkhana in order to get a visa—they provided an address in Pakistan. You railed against the Americans right from the start. You wanted to support the Islamic fighters. You had already established contact with them in Hamburg, which is a hive of Islamic militant activity. Most Afghani refugees in Peshawar are Taliban.

You were probably a go-between for the groups in Hamburg and the fighters in Peshawar. You wanted to facilitate jihad. You took part in demonstrations where calls to war were made and American flags were burned, where our president was burned in effigy. You took part in meetings and weapons training. You wanted to go with them to Afghanistan. The road from Peshawar to Afghanistan is the supply route of the Taliban. It goes directly to Tora Bora, where your leader, the head of Al Qaida, Osama bin Laden, is hiding out. From there it would be on to Kabul, the final leg, where you'd retake power. You wanted to fight Americans, to kill Americans. More likely the Americans would have killed you. See, you got lucky. Nothing's going to happen to you. You just have to tell us what you were planning. Who your comrades were. And, most important, who the leader was.

Rashid can see how this is supposed to go. But at the same time he can see his hands cuffed in front of his stomach and, below, his feet, his clenched toes, and the chains around his feet. It's hot. The wood floor is scratched. He's disappointed the story is over. It's a good story, and all the details fit cleanly together. He'd like to hear to more. There's a lead there, a path through the confusion. He need only follow it, make the correct turn, and everything will go smoothly. He can't stand any longer. He needs to lay down and think things over. He'd been pulled into the war. That's the way forward, straight-ahead. It's clear. But it's also a one-way road. He's Indian, and Muslim. America is against Muslims. He is one. He wanted to go to Afghanistan because of Mirgul, Mirgul with his prayer rug. Mirgul, the Americans—something's not right here. *America good*, he had said. He, Rashid, is against the Americans. *They kill people but they are no terminators*. They're blowhards. They subjugate the whole world. You have to defend yourself against them. They beat him. They're his enemy. They imprisoned him. He's tired. He has to fight. He has to defend himself. He wants to sleep. There's no way he can betray those men. He's a warrior. He must not give in. He lifts his head.

I didn't pay for Mirgul's flight. I just loaned him the money. Maybe he betrayed me because of that.

The names, says the voice. The names, repeats the interpreter in German. He tries to remember. The people in Peshawar. Nothing but names, funny names. The barber shop was called Amjal. The mosque was called Mahabat. Then there was the bazaar and Storyteller Street. From Peshawar to Tora Bora and Jalalabad—another crazy name—and then to Kabul. He just needs to get his bearings—the road is all mapped out. *Go on*, says the voice. Rashid cringes as he takes a blow to the back of the head and a shot to each kidney; his knees buckle and slam into the floor. A kick to the back and he sprawls forward. *Okay, that's enough.* He feels hands grab him under his arms. They raise him to his feet. He totters, manages to stand, feels the trickle down his leg, the sticky moisture—please don't let them see it. She's talking, a woman. He can't see her—please don't let her see it. It's a sharp voice, mother-like, strong. *Mr. Bakhrani*, she says. *Herr* Bakhrani, says the interpreter. You could be with us for a long time. It's up to you. Your time here could be much more comfortable. We could extend your *recreation time*, for instance. The woman pauses. *More sports, more showers*, she says. Perhaps a chance to socialize with other prisoners. Downgraded to level-four security—you'd get to eat and live together with others. Video games. And then perhaps your release. But you have to work with us. You have to cooperate.

It's dead quiet. Work with us. *You have to cooperate.*

Rashid's head is pounding. *Much more comfortable.* He gets it. The woman's voice rings in his ears. *And then perhaps your release.* She would help him. He's no terrorist. He just needs to cooperate. He can see trees, a tree-lined street, leaves strewn on the sidewalk, crates in front of the store, the open door to his building, the staircase. That's where he belongs. It's simple. He just needs to make it clear to her. He can no longer stand. His wrists are bleeding. He whispers. I'm a German tourist. He coughs, clears his throat, it blares in his ears. I'm not Rashid Bakhrani. I never wanted to go to Afghanistan. My name is Leo. Leo Erxleben. I was on vacation in Pakistan with a friend. We were in Lahore. Peshawar was an accident—we got on the wrong bus. I wanted to go back. But there was a demonstration. I had nothing to do with it. The Pakistani police arrested me. I don't even know anyone in Peshawar. You can ask my parents. I'm not Muslim. I've never prayed. I want to go home. *Mr. Bakhrani*, says the woman. This is not the right way. If you aren't willing to help us, you'll never get home. We're after the terrorists. We know who you are. I thought you would help us identify them. Think. You need a break. *Recreation. Air conditioning. Showers.* The interpreter is silent. *Please translate*, she says. Air conditioning, the interpreter says in German. Showers.

Okay. This is the officer again. *Cooler*, he says. The red-faced MP steps in front of him, grabs him by the shirt front and lifts his chin. The other one, behind him, puts the goggles over his head. Rashid doubles over in the dark. Next come the ear plugs. He lurches, hears himself scream, goes limp. A hand claps over his mouth and shoves the scream back down his throat. His arms are lifted, the handcuffs dig into his skin, he's pulled straight upright, his feet drag, boots kick at his calves and heels. Then his feet are kicked out from under him and he is hanging, swinging, a sack, ever emptier and lighter. He grazes a hard barrier, they maneuver him through a narrow passageway. They dump him to the ground and begin to undo him. He can hear again, he sees a bare poured-concrete floor, he sees them taking off the chains around his ankles, unlocking the handcuffs. They kneel next to him and take off the straps. There are four of them. They stand up, looking down at him on the dirty floor. The place looks like a bathroom, windowless, white tiles, two green buckets against the wall, a door to a stall, cold ceiling lights, everything cold looking. He props himself up. His wrists are bloody. He looks up. *Your turn*, one of them says. Rashid doesn't recognize him. His face seems far away. He's huge, a tall, handsome, angular man with dark stubble and small, round glasses. The man looks down at him. *Time to strip*. The face comes closer. *Take that off*, he says, tearing at his collar. The face is very close now, gray eyes behind the glasses; first the eyes, then his lips retreat, his teeth appear, his mouth opens and he yells: *Take off your shirt*.

Rashid tries to grab the hem of his shirt. His hands are numb. He slowly lifts his arms and starts to pull up the shirt. His shoulders are stiff and every inch is a struggle. Finally his head passes through the collar and he can see his own pale stomach. He pulls at the shirt, fighting the pins and needles in his hands, forces his head the rest of the way through, drops his arms to his lap and pulls his hands through the inside-out sleeves. Three soldiers are leaning against the wall, arms crossed in front of their chests, each with one foot propped at knee-height on the wall behind him. The one in glasses stands in front of him: *Perfect, and now the pants you pissed*. The others laugh, and one of them switches the foot he's got propped against the wall. Rashid goes to his knees and unbuttons his pants, stands up, and steps out of them. He leaves the rubber sandals under his pants and the floor is cold. Rashid looks at the orange clothes next to his feet, thinks of the heat outside, the shower stall with the green door, *recreation, air conditioning, showers*. He waits, feeling that the man in camo next to him wants him to wait. His wet underwear is his last layer of protection. He doesn't know what underpants are called in English, but he knows he won't hear the final order as long as he has them on. Without looking up he sees the big guy nod his chin. The three MPs step away from the wall and the giant takes a step closer to Rashid: *Everything*, he shouts, *don't waste our time*. He kicks the orange clothes to the side. Rashid peels his underwear down, below the knees; it's sticky and he has to keep pushing it down, bending over, staggering. As he steps on the wet cloth, the contents of the green buckets fly in his direction—water splashes over his whole body. He cringes, puts his hands in front of his face. They lift him up. The stall is open. It swallows him up. He crashes into a wall.

Walls all around. Gray metal walls, covered with a grayish white crust. His back burns, his wet skin sticks to the stuff on the walls, rips as he rights himself. He has to stand upright, his arms pressed to his sides, in order to avoid touching the walls. He's in a freezer. He can hear himself breathing, in, out, and each time he does he can see a puff of fog blow from his mouth. Steam comes off his skin. The warmth of his breath dissipates as it hits the walls. The only thing alive in here is him. No handle. He pounds on the wall he thinks is the door. It resounds with a dull echo. He has to stay upright but he can't stand still, he doesn't stand still—he dances. The cold is coming through his feet, from the floor, the same poured concrete surface as outside. He hops around. Everything is fluttering around. He has his fists crossed on his chest but begins to move them around, rubbing his collarbones. He wants to rub his chest and stomach and arms with his palms, but he doesn't dare open his fists or risk straightening out his elbows. The walls are too close. They emanate cold. Air conditioning. They will let him out. He shivers. He has to bounce and stomp. He tries to stop shivering. It gets slower. The walls seem to get closer. He presses his hands to his throat, clenches his jaw closed. His feet dance up and down like pistons. They are pumping out the cold. He wants to jump so he is totally off the cold floor for at least a second. But he doesn't have the strength. Suddenly he stops hopping. He stands on his toes and drums his fists on the walls. There's no space for a backswing. His fists burn. They are blue. Blue and red. His whole body has a blue sheen. The walls have gotten whiter. Up high there's a grille circling the freezer, horizontal slats. He stops pounding on the wall. He can't control his hands anymore, the shivering is too overwhelming. He has to ball himself up, hold on, thigh pressed to his calf and stomach pressed to his thigh and arms wrapped around his knees. He tries to crouch. His knees hit one wall and his back scrapes against another. Too tight. He's stuck. The ice eats into his skin. Everything is slippery and there's nothing to hold onto to hoist himself up. His feet are pressed forward and his muscles are too weak to get them back under him. He can't move, can't lift himself back up. He's too far down. He presses his hands against the side walls, trying to get leverage. His arms are too weak. They shake. They slip. He can't feel his feet anymore. He leans his head back. He sits still. The freezer motor hums. He can hear his head vibrating against the wall. His feet are gone. The pain burns out, fading from red-hot to ashen white. His shivering gets weaker and weaker.

The door is at his back. They catch him. A blue blanket, a stretcher, straps. He starts to shiver again. His hands tingle, needles, and where his feet were, daggers of ice. Someone rubs his chest and pounds on it, dull thuds. The stretcher cradles his raw, scraped back. Then the burning and shaking yields to a humming vibration, he's rolling on a gurney. The floor is smooth, like at the infirmary; he's being pushed along, saved. He doesn't have to do anything more. He lies there, gliding along with his eyes closed. Reality seeps in rosy drops through his eyelids, through the blanket, into his limbs, like steam slowly softening the glaring, icy light of his day dreams. At the same time, he hears the regular clop-clop of their strides, now stopping short, now speeding up again, slight dizziness, a thwack, and he's arrived, somewhere safe, somewhere—he doesn't care where. Sleep. A chance to give up. Leave everything behind, defrost, forget the bindings holding him down, forget his feet, his back, the stinging and burning, the memories. The doctor hovers over him: We'll use the crane, he says, now that you're circumcized you fit perfectly in the container and we'll ship you. He smiles beneath his white turban, his facial features are soft, dark—it's *Baba's* face. A horn blows and the Ferris wheel jerks into motion, the scent of roasted almonds and fuel oil and harbor water in the air. Rashid is going up, floating. *Baba* waves, his face receding, and yells: I'll pick you up. A swing, the container turns, beneath him the ocean, the railing, the deck, the sailors. The carriage swivels, they stretch out their arms, they grab him, they call: *up now pisshead.* They remove the restraints. He punches out. They rip off the blanket and yank him upright. The room is small, low, a pair of black chairs sit against the wall. He is sitting naked on the gurney with his feet hanging over the edge, still blue. At his feet are his orange clothes and, in a dark lump on top, his underwear.

Wanna wear this? Rashid looks up and recognizes

the big head and the voice—*don't tell us fairytales*—as the officer stands beside the gurney and points at the wet clothes. He's dizzy, the waves are still lapping back and forth beneath him, the gray linoleum floor, the orange outfit, the boots—three pairs; at the head of the bed standing with their legs wide apart are two soldiers, the tall one with glasses and a black one. *Okay, you don't want to*, says the officer, *let's make an eagle*, quick. Rashid is pushed from the gurney, spun around, and smacks the floor on his stomach with the heap of clothes right in front of his face. One of them is kneeling on his back, another kicks his feet apart. His hands are pulled above his head, palms up. *Don't move*, growls the officer. Rashid doesn't squirm, he presses his cold body against the cold linoleum. He hears his teeth chattering, footsteps and scraping noises. He wheezes from the pressure on his rib cage and finally jerks when something is pressed into the soles of his feet and then into the palms of his hands. He only starts to scream when the bruised pressure points start to bore into his feet like broom handles and seem to drill his hands into place. He manages to crane his head and sees the legs of a chair on his hands, and the boots and camo pants of someone sitting on it. *You say you know English, nazi?* The officer's voice comes from behind him—he's sitting on the chair on Rashid's feet. Rashid fills his lungs, his ribs pressing against the floor, the smell of piss from the orange pile. His throat rattles when he breathes out. *Tell me, smart guy*, the officer's voice booms through the void, *did you deal with the Taliban?* Rashid tries to nod, his cheek bounces against the floor. *Yes, he did*, says a different voice, higher, the black soldier. *Did you deal with the Al-Qaida terrorists?* Yes, Rashid hears it ring out crystal clear, *yes. I did*, he adds. He hears himself speaking English and pictures himself in the second to last row in the classroom of the school on

Friedrichstrasse, in Hamburg. He can see the wooden desks. It's his own voice, rushing through his body from his hands and feet and finally whistling out of his lungs. *Fine, did you kill Americans?* Kill. Kill Americans. Now Rashid sees himself on the floor, understands he's the eagle. Mama always liked that song by Steve Miller, *fly like an eagle 'til I'm free.* He needs to stick to the truth. It's hard to shake his head. *No.* This time it's not his voice he hears. It's the black guy. He has understood. *He says no,* the guy says. *But you want to kill Americans,* calls out the officer. Rashid breathes in, *yes,* he cries out, though it sounds weak. *Yes,* he repeats, the pain still driving through his feet, but now gone in his hands, now just aching. Rashid lays there. He's made it.

They tell him to *stand up.* It's as if he's never known another language. They say stand up and he stands up, though slowly and awkwardly. Too slowly, but the kick he takes is as routine to him as dropping change in his pocket would normally be. It's a clear, transparent language. Its tones and intonations and the gestures and actions and impressions they've left on his body—it all fits together somehow. It all makes sense. He just needs to work at it. His limbs will only move with patience and the application of force. His joints only very slowly remember their function, to allow his bulky bones to bend. His spine is hunched, his rib cage stiff and aching. He puts his feet on the floor and shifts his weight from foot to foot, the stinging pain of one answered by the dull throb of the other. It's logical, the predictable result of a simple cause. As he stands up, he feels as if nothing else can happen to him. It's difficult to stand, but he does it. He braces himself against the gurney and nobody tries to stop him. The black guy lines the chairs back up against the wall. The officer stands in the middle of the room, hands clasped behind him, his right boot tapping on the floor. Rashid waits for instructions. The guy with glasses sits with one leg on the edge of the gurney and watches Rashid work his way to his feet. They've shown him the way, with words and blows, with hot and cold. He just needs to go along, follow the trail. He understands, he agrees.

He's supposed to put on his clothes. That means he has to bend over again, even more, drop to his knees because he can't flex his upper body, can't put weight on his feet, can't bend his fingers. It takes time. To get into his underpants he has to stand first on one foot and then on the other. So far so good. He hikes the sticky cold underwear up his legs. It catches on his balls and then slips wetly over his cheeks as Rashid goes to lift the orange pants. The three soldiers look on silently. They can tell he's cooperating, how well it's working. Rashid braces himself on the frame of the gurney, puts his weight on the leg he's already slipped into the pants. He pulls the cloth with one hand while he maneuvers his other foot into the remaining leg hole. He wobbles and the MP with glasses thoughtfully puts a hand on his shoulder to hold him up. *Come on, chicken*, he barks. There's a metal rattling; the black MP has the *three-piece* in his hand. Rashid puts his forearms together and they do the rest: shirt over the head, clamps, straps fastened, handcuffs and leg irons, rubber sandals. The only thing he has to do himself is walk, *head down*, between the black MP and the one in glasses. The officer is gone. For the first time Rashid can see the smooth linoleum floor of the corridors. He tries to put his weight only on the outer edges of his feet. They turn, there's a steel door, a wood floor, and finally he reemerges into the light and can smell the perfumed sweat of interrogation. They let go of him.

Only faint murmurs seep through the wall of

light. The voices are busy speaking to each other, far away
from the void surrounding him. Rashid stands there alone
in the gleaming emptiness. He wants to talk, he's waiting
to be questioned. Time passes, time stands still, everything
is a fever dream. The only thing giving him any sense of
orientation is the stabbing pain in his feet. His head rocks
back and forth like a pendulum. When he closes his eyes
and lets his eyelids filter the beams of light, he's struck by
the image of shooting stars falling towards earth, blowing
him apart as they streak by, sweeping him along in their
trail. He's got to keep his eyes open, focus on his body and
his immediate surroundings. His orange outfit gleams like
the red wasteland behind his eyelids. The material is sticking to his skin with sweat, glowing, though his bare hands
are still blue icicles. Rashid waits, listens, squints. The light
pours over him. He recognizes the voices of the officers,
the woman's voice and the nasal twang of the storyteller:
Tora Bora, weapons, contacts, logistics. Chairs are moved
around and he flinches. His leg irons rattle against the
floor. He staggers, gets himself together, and stands still
again. A shadow passes through the intense cloud of light.
Rashid's muscles are beginning to freeze up. The handcuffs
are cutting into the ripped skin of his wrists. Then a silent
blow and everything disappears as he blacks out. A black
curtain has fallen. Silence. Exhale. A window opens in the
dark. Beyond it is cold, grainy light and right in the
middle, looking in through the window, is a huge head,
the gaunt face and long beard of a cleric beneath a white
turban, sickly, familiar. He looks at Rashid through black
eyes, the fleshy lips below his huge nose open in an expres-
sion of pain. He's speaking in a foreign language. Do you
know this man? It's the interpreter's voice, the halting
German.

Oh yes, he knows him; he knows himself, he

knows the way, racing past, snow on the wall. He's been asleep for a while. The dream-images light up and then are extinguished: tunics, Kalashnikovs, checkered Palestinian scarves, homemade rockets, flags, posters, Arabic symbols, Indian symbols, ammunition depots, rooms, house doors, streets, carpets, chairs and always faces, the faces of middle eastern clerics, western agents. He'd seen them all before, been everywhere. He had extensive travels behind him and had walked until his feet couldn't go any farther, swollen and rubbed raw. At some points he says yes, at others no; sometimes he forgets to answer at all. In the half-light that fills the room from the funnel-shaped beam of the projector, he can make out the shadowy shapes of his interrogators—dappled light on their uniforms, the compact silhouette of the officer, the light-colored shirts, the woman's puffy hair helmet. He falls into a dream. Suddenly he wakes up on the floor of a bus driving on a raised highway, barren land and dirty gray buildings below. Palm trees line the streets, women's veils blow in the breeze. Changing lanes, swerving, a cracking noise, and a floorboard smacks his face. They help him up, roughly, his whole body in pain, and set him on his feet. The questions are driving him crazy but he has to answer to keep the images moving. No, the Al-Kud mosque in St. Georg— Hamburg—he doesn't recognize. He does recognize the mosque in the Altona section of the city. He's never been to Marienstrasse in the suburb of Harburg. He's been in the mosque in Peshawar—it's called Mahabat. He met the man in the tie in Hamburg, Omar or Habib or Nazir. The pickup truck's in a weapons depot in Peshawar. He ran into the man in the brown suit and Palestinian scarf on the bus from Lahore to Peshawar—or maybe it was in the air- port in Delhi. The mullah with the thick-rimmed glasses gave a sermon in Peshawar, either at the mosque or at a demonstration. The fat guy with the graying beard he's never seen before. He's never been to the cafeteria at the institute of technology in Harburg. The Taliban commander with the ammunition belt used to come into the barber shop—Mustafa or Sultan or Reza. That young warrior with the pockmarked face and an assault rifle used to come with him. Yes, but without the rifle—he's a volunteer fighter. The man in the dark tunic is a volunteer. Yes, he himself is also a volunteer.

At some point the lights in the room blaze back on. The voices interrupt each other impatiently, pressuring, digging deeper, making suggestions, then stopping and waiting. They specify targets, locations, connections, weapons, names and more names. The interpreter stutters along a few steps behind, Rashid's ear drums vibrate, and he talks in order to stay awake and keep from keeling over. He carried messages for Reza and Ali, letters of introduction. He wanted to fight. There was a plan. They wanted to meet up with Mirgul's father, Shah or Munawar or Hakim. They wanted to transport mines or grenade launchers over the border, either in the pickup or on donkeys or both. They were going to put together a team in Jalalabad, set up a storage depot for explosives—he wasn't sure where—and hit American bases. He didn't know which ones, maybe in town, maybe at the airport, the one near the refugee camp, next to the bridge over the river, in the south, in the north, the small one or the big one—of course, the big one. The big river in the north is the Kabul river—how could the Kabul river flow through Jalalabad? Rashid begins to cry. He's lost. He doesn't know what's going on anymore. He can't stand up any longer. He entered the war but he was never in Afghanistan. He is supposed to help the Americans but he doesn't want to give anything away. He has forgotten the names. He's an

Islamic fighter but he doesn't know what his orders were. He had planned assassinations, but he doesn't know which ones. He can barely talk anymore. He's not a tourist. He's a terrorist. He wants to prove it, but he never saw battle. He can't keep his eyes open any longer. He lied. It's his fault. He can't feel his feet anymore, can't feel his hands. He is a prisoner of war. He wants to sleep, he wants to fight.

How many fighters were there? What country were they from? Were there Saudis there? Syrians, Egyptians, Algerians, Lebanese, or Iranians? Rashid lets his head dangle so low that his chin hits his ribs. They need him. He doesn't have to answer. He doesn't speak their language but understands anyway. They slam their fists on the table. They shout. Were there cell phones? Were there satellite phones? He is silent and listens to their desperation. Were there maps? He thinks of his tattered *Lonely Planet* guide and wonders to himself where he could be now. He sees the splotchy pictures, the brown uplands of the Khyber Pass and the green depths of the valleys beyond the border, the road extending into the distance. He listens to his frantic breathing. Mirgul on the bus at the Shangla Pass. Snowfall in the Himalayas. The broad foreheads of the sherpas. The footpaths of the merchants. Terraced pastures. Tibetan prayer rugs. Symbols chiseled into the rocks along the trail. His eyes soar over green-brown valleys, lightheaded from the thin air, his body trailing along behind. He just needs to lay down on the ground and let himself roll down the bottomless incline, rolling, rolling. But they grab him, hold him up, and yank his head up. Were there drugs? Were they used or stockpiled or sold? Rashid says nothing. This is the way to go about it, he decides. He doesn't know anything. The twang of the storyteller becomes pinched and squawky. Does the name

Hekmatyar mean anything to you? What about the name
Dostum? Ismail Khan? Rashid doesn't say no and doesn't
say yes. The MPs thump him in the back, pull his arms
away from his body and then punch him just beneath his
rib cage. Were people praying? How did they pray? The
woman screeches, the interpreter stutters. What was the
organization called? Prophet's Army? Hezb-e-Islami, Sepa
I Shahaba, Islamic Jihad? It's so easy just to remain silent.
He's able to talk but doesn't want to. Who were these men?
Are you a member of the Muslim Brotherhood?

      Rashid falls asleep standing up. He answers in his
sleep. I know why I'm here. The time, the chains, the pain.
I've finally figured out why I'm here. I'm an enemy, a
dangerous enemy. This is war. There are secrets. I'm not
going to squeal. It's a life and death struggle. That's why
I'm here. I'm a warrior. I know what side I'm on. I'm not
going to negotiate. I want to kill Americans. The war is
not over. The island, the cage, the seeming eternity. He's
awake now. He lifts his head and looks at the light. *Yes, I
am a Muslim*, he says. He says it in good English. *You
joined the Muslim Brotherhood*, asks the deep voice. *Yes*,
Rashid says. It hurts to talk. *The group had no other name
than Muslim Brotherhood?* No, says Rashid. *You wanted to
fight with them?* Rashid nods. *Jihad*, he says. He had never
used this word before. He understands their language and
they understand him. He's empty. Everything's been said,
spewed out as if from a burst valve. All that's left is a
charred shell, burned out, wilted skin, ash. He's tired. He's
a warrior. Neon-red rings pulse behind his eyelids, expanding outward in concentric circles and becoming red floodlights, rings of fire, Ferris wheels, dimming slowing as they
expand outward, until the last of their life and heat flicker
out. He can make out the darkness beyond. The peaceful-
ness. He's fought long enough. He's ready to give up,

anticipating it. He wants to die. He stops moving, lets it happen. The darkness expands. It's coming to him. It descends on him. He crawls under it like heavy blanket. Time stops. He dies. He hovers. The Ferris wheel takes him, whirring as it spins; he rises, gliding into space. Way down below him they are bustling about, pushing and shoving, their commanders far away and peaceful. *War is over.*

When he returns to the ground, the shadows are receding. The sun has woken him up and set fire to his pain. All around he hears knocking and grinding, rattling and buzzing. He blinks, chain links prick into his eyes, he closes them tight and sees for a fleeting moment the ocean. Waves lap quietly at his feet. Then they're gone and the ponderous voice of the muezzin rises above the cages.

IV. *Death*. Luck

When toothpaste dries in the sun, it gets brittle. It congeals, begins to crack, shrivels. And it loses its color. It turns from light green—the color it emerges from the tube marked *Government Issue Mint Toothpaste*—to talc white. Finally the surface turns to powder and can be blown away. A boot, gallows, a circle, waves, letters, numbers— everything disappears as white dust in days or weeks.

He kneels at the back wall of the cage and rubs the crumbled lines off the floor with the palms of his hands. In the stalls around him, they're doing their routine again on their towels. Rashid has been lying on his mattress since *dinner*, thinking about whether he should stand up. It's hard on him, because he has an invisible hole inside him, and only food can for short periods fill it. As soon as he gets up, he feels the ever-expanding hollowness between his pelvis and neck. But everything is functioning normally; only his knee hurts against the hard concrete. He works slowly and precisely, and deliberates over each motion. He wipes the mix of dirt and chalk off on his pants and unscrews the top from the tube. He's careful not to waste any of the paste. A small, viscous drop on his pointer finger is enough for a letter, or half that for the letter "i." He lays each line with the edge of his finger, then goes back over it with his fingertip creating all the shapes he needs in finger-width strips of color on the concrete, long, angled, across and one rounded: K-I-R-A-T. Up to now the MPs haven't discovered his designs. They're suspicious of letters. They find meanings in them. There are "I"s and "A"s everywhere: Rashid, Tarik, Kirat, Islam. Letters shaken up in a dice cup, secret combinations. Tarik and Islam—the *chaplain*, Muhammad Halabi-Islam—are gone. Left are Rashid and Kirat the lizard.

When he first saw the lizard, it was on the base of the plywood wall behind his cage, hanging there like a neon-green letter, head down, glimmering, rigid. For a second he was startled. It was pretty, as if from another world. It didn't belong in a prison. He stared at it, as if he could hold it in place with his eyes, and stayed in the same position he'd been in when he first spotted it there, squatting on his mattress—since his first interrogation he'd been unable to sit on concrete anymore—his head turned halfway around over his shoulder. He thought he saw one of its eyes move like a rotating mechanical ball sticking out of an otherwise dead surface. There was nothing to suggest a heart was beating or lungs breathing inside the contours of its form, and yet it was a complete living thing, self-sufficient and distinct. The shape of its body—with no neck, coming to a point at the end of its head, its tapered tail beyond the splayed legs longer than its head and body put together—made it look like an arrow pointing to the ground. Its long tail was an odd piece of decoration, seemingly superfluous and fragile, but it made the reptile a stubbornly unmistakable creature. A lizard. As long as a measuring stick. The same cool, shimmering color he imagined the nearby ocean to be, near the shore, where the golden sand lightened the shade of the water; bright flecks glittering amidst the turquoise depths, and golden stripes running from the lizard's shoulders to its jaws with that same shimmering light.

After a while, Rashid discovered that waves actually twitched on the surface. Tiny glittering shadows would wash the spots from the skin and then make them reappear. A light show with its source inside the animal itself. He stared at it, and forgot about himself. The changes on its skin seemed to be trying to communicate something. He wanted to understand. The motions of this motionless creature must hold some meaning, some promise. The wandering changes of color seemed to increase. Then they started to synchronize. And then suddenly one big wave pulsed across its whole body, washing away the green color. It became paler, warmer, the entire animal seemed to disappear and then reappear. As Rashid watched, the ocean green turned to light brown. The lizard melted into the plywood. It still hadn't moved. It was magic. The light flecks were still there, and still shimmering. Rashid bent forward until he could see through the chain links without seeing the wire, and just as his face was about to touch the fence, the tail whipped silently to the side and the arrow shot off. Just above the ground the lizard stopped and looked around, then it was off into the grass. Its light brown body dashed through the blades of grass and disappeared. Rashid's heart pounded, flitting in his chest like a bird held in a fist.

Since then it comes and visits him whenever he wants it to. At first he would stare for hours at the plywood wall. He was the only one who could see the arrow with limbs and the long tip, holding itself there motionless among the shifting shadows. He spoke secretly to it, and all the voices in his head got quieter. Then he had recreated the arrow shape in his cage. But the pale mint-colored toothpaste, which contained some of the same ocean green pigmentation of the lizard's skin, faded gradually until all that was left on the ground was a chalky, white line. At night the line glows dully, as everything white does because of the floodlights. The chalk arc is still reminiscent of the shape of Kirat's body. Rashid had named the lizard that. He tells it what's going on in the prison camp. Whatever he describes and explains seems to unburden him. It's a quiet, difficult process with lots of starts and stops. He describes how the showers look and how long the spray lasts before you have to push the button again to restart it; how the Uzbek reminds him of a pit bull; that the guy hates the black soldiers and barks at them; that as he blows his nose he holds one nostril closed and blows out the other, leaving the snot hanging on the fence wire. He tells the lizard how he collects himself the fluff that blows into his cage from the grass and has built a mound out of it, how soft it feels when he lets it trickle through his fingers. He doesn't talk about how he thought about the fluff mound when he was showering, when he was trying to think of a face and realized it was gone, or that his cock hadn't reacted. Or about the interrogations that seem to continue even in the cages, the negotiations. It wouldn't understand. It's just a lizard. It's enough to be able to talk about basic things, things that belong to somebody else, not to him or to the lizard. It almost gives him the feeling of being surrounded by reality. Once in a while he reads to it from the Koran.

He looks at the dried lettering. Backwards it reads T-A-R-I-K. The name is odd and generic at the same time, just like his own. Sometimes for a second he remembers what it was like to be Rashid. It tethers him to the world even when he feels he can no longer stand to interact with himself or the world. A round, pulsing sensation hits him, weak and distant, like someone waving to him long after he's said goodbye. The memories are weaker and come less frequently now, which is good. It hurts to be reminded of the easy relationship he had with himself. He hasn't heard his own name in ages. To the interrogators he's *Mr. Bakhrani*. To the MPs he's *sand nigger* or *towelhead* or *fucking terrorist*. Outside, the escorts call him *guy* or *man* or *two-O-four*. The number 204 is stitched on the light blue band practically fused to his wrist. It's the number he has to write on the lined, postcard-sized letters he sends home: Detainee JJJ A204, 160 Camp X-Ray, Washington, DC, 20353, USA. The Uzbek in the next cage just grunts when he wants to talk to Rashid. It sounds like *hoj*. Or sometimes he says *schorrmen*, supposed to sound like *German*, before launching into a rant about the food or the noise or a black MP. Most of the time he sits on the bare floor with his back to Rashid's cage and his head between his knees, mumbling. He beats his fists on the concrete floor, left, right, left, right, in a halting rhythm interrupted by pauses. Once in a while he jumps to his feet and rams his head into the wall, once, twice, three times. The chain link fence clangs each time until the Uzbek stops, panting and twitching, his arms hanging limp, before throwing himself onto his mattress as if it's quitting time after a long day's work. It isn't long before he's mumbling again. At night Rashid sometimes wakes with a start, the fence clanging in the gloom, and he himself starts to talk, too, to whisper to Kirat: There he goes again. Everybody here is crazy. I'm crazy. Maybe you can tell me where this will all end. You live here, after all. You should get out of here. The toothpaste glows. Kirat listens from outside. Nothing between them but air.

The buckets have been changed. Shadows no longer play on the plywood wall. An artificial dawn is about to break. The path still has a tired dirt color to it. It's empty as it always is during prayers. At some point the MPs retreat, driven by the will of Allah's oranges. Suleyman had screamed at one during midday prayers for noisily dragging a couple of *three-pieces* through the yard. A patrol had beaten him in his cage until he couldn't stand. By evening he was gone; they had broken his arm. But that was a while ago. It's quieter in the camp these days. Even when another person hangs himself there's no big uproar. The loud ones disappear. You never know why until they return—except for Tarik and Suleyman, they usually return to their original cages. They're just quieter. All the crazy ones still fidget, but they fidget in a more contained fashion—their ticks slow down and diversify. Like the Uzbek. His thick head still crashes against the wall, and he still rages and spits through the fence. Others rage and spit through the chain-link fencing, too—it's just what they do. They get punished. Their privileges are diminished and then increased again: one shower a week, then back to two showers a week. They eat and sleep and are taken away and brought back. Nothing else. Everything's fine outside.

But there's crushing pressure inside, an invisible, nervous, crushing pressure. The choir of voices bothers him, the mumbling and the getting up and down. He squats at the head of his mattress and leans his head carefully against the fence looking at his work. He wants quiet. He needs to protect himself. He needs to think, to find his way. They are at *Ibrahim*, and again *Ibrahim, innaka hamidun majid.* They're almost to the end. But he knows the praying won't stop anymore than the cursing and growling and rattling—it all gets in here, and his cage is just too small. They cough and snarl and snore. They shit and piss and jack off in the wash buckets. They crouch and gawk. Sometimes they are silent—but even the silence presses through the cage walls. And the MPs come by, pull chains through the fencing and storm in, stomping their feet, trampling on the towels, spilling the buckets. They

throw the doors closed, the shrill sound of the locks echoing in the bruised emptiness of his body. The noise and
chatter is constant. Always pressing in on him, making
him wince, making him jump, startling him, like the mosquitoes that stick themselves to his body and hum in his
ear—all of it inescapable. *A 's-salamu alaykum.* They all
stand up. The hot air buzzes with scraping and rustling.
The loudspeaker crackles. The sun has made another complete pass over the prison camp. Every day it wraps around
the camp like a new fence. Every time the lights go on at
night, the cage has gotten smaller. The lights go on.

   The colors seep out as if everything's been dipped
in bleach. The pattern of the wire fencing is cast on the
ground. The crosshatched patterns overlap making a faded
carpet of shadows. Once the twilight fades this pattern of
distorted black diamonds remains on the bluish concrete
until morning prayers, a tightly meshed series of grids one
on top of the other. K-I-R-A-T. The letters smeared on the
ground between the head of his mattress and the waste
bucket have dulled. The rounded part of the R is the last
bit with a green sheen to it. He misses the bright shapes.
The character of the whole cage has changed. The letters
hardly bring the lizard to mind. Instead he sees it as T-A-
R-I-K. Tarik even writes his name backwards. He had
spelled it out in Arabic for Rashid once, his finger writing
in the air from right to left—which is how he reads the
Koran, too, from right to left. Rashid could barely remember what Tarik looked like anymore. His grimacing face
smashed against the fence was the only image he had. For
a while he had continued to talk with him even after he
was gone. The voice in which Tarik answered—after a long
pause, in his broken English—sounded strange.
Sometimes he still heard it. And sometimes other voices
joined in. The voices would float in from outside and

gather beneath his skin: *If we get your help, we'll help you,*
The Fire be your dwelling place: You will dwell therein
forever, ash'hadu anna Muhammadan 'abduhu wa rasuluh,
ask your interrogators, answer us or you will never see your
parents again, head down, He is Oft-Forgiving and Most
Merciful, ask your interrogators. Far too near, far too loud.
So now he's taken to talking to himself to drown out the
voices. Kirat's always around, but always silent. He stretches out his hand, traces the R, and licks his finger. A warped
grid of diamonds is cast on his arm, the open spaces glowing violet from the flood lights. He sees the silhouette of
his arm against the bare plywood wall.

    The steps come along the path fast. They belong
to the doctor. Rashid swallows the chewing gum flavor of
the toothpaste. A walkie-talkie beeps: *two-two-six,* it crackles. *Yes,* says the doctor behind him, *I'm on my way.* The
footsteps thud in Rashid's eardrums, reverberating like an
echo. Dirt crumbles on Rashid's tongue. To the first flood-
light belongs the stealthy walk of the Islam-MP, the chaplain Mohammad. Also the scorching Arabic melody near
Tarik's cage and the slow English words in the same voice:
Be as patient as possible, read, read every day, it will help you,
the hollow dark face behind the chain links. Then this face
disappears as well. The book sits in the shadow cast by the
waste bucket: *This is the glorious Book, In it is guidance sure,*
without doubt, to those who fear Allah. It's green and white
like the shower stalls and the toothpaste. *Read the last*
suras, they're short, they are right for prayer. Rashid is too
heavy to stand up. It's too much effort—always the same
pages, and the pages all the same. On every page evil is
punished and good rewarded. Allah is all-knowing. The
sentences are so long, the plots go around in circles, tough
but bland; from paradise to hell and back again, full of
dead words, such as righteous, blasphemous, reprobate,

and humble. Allah wants a victimized camel's leg back up to strength, wants the left foot and the right hand of an evil man hacked off—or the right foot and the left hand. It's a book of fairytales for children and old or stupid people. It doesn't belong in a prison. It doesn't fit in with the plastic plates and latrines, loudspeakers and floodlights. It only fits in with the prisoners, filled with words and names and tribes and cities and battles, a huge assembly under open skies—and at the end Allah can somehow distinguish between the believers and the non-believers, leaving the believers snickering at the non-believers. Rashid knows he's evil, knows he's a non-believer. He only seems like a believer when he reads the book; it reads to him like a letter. But now he can't read, can't stand. He doesn't want to do anything but be still and talk, talk with the *chaplain*, talk with the *interrogators*, talk with Kirat.

Dark lines of shadows fall in across the toothpaste letters—just like the black bars blotting out German words in the letters *Baba* sends, *cleared by U.S. Forces*. Rashid closes his eyes; the light and dark strips are reversed until they dissipate. So, Rashid says to Kirat, the doctor is here. He slows down and pauses. Behind Rashid the Uzbek is pounding his fists on the ground softly and irregularly. Across the way an orange is moaning. It's a long, drawn-out tone, then a pause, then it starts up again with a grinding, sing-song sound. The thin curving sound of the moan makes him think of the shape of Kirat's body. Rashid opens his eyes. Kirat's name is staring him in the face. He gathers his strength and takes a deep breath; his chest heaves and his stomach sucks in. He tries to speak. The new guy across the path is already gone, he says. He wouldn't walk even though he was capable of walking, so they took him away on a stretcher. Once again Islam hasn't come to see him.

He remains still. He sits with his hands backward on the mattress, fighting the urge to pull up his knees and wrap his arms around them. He knows that when he touches and holds himself, he feels the emptiness in his gut spread out all the way from his haunches to his throat. It eats at him and he feels lighter even though he's gotten fat and out of shape, plumped up by the food put in his inert body. He tries to play up his weight, moving sluggishly and deliberately. He just lets the soccer ball sit there in the playpen during recreation time. He lumbers around the little concrete courtyard along the fence that rings it. He can take up to 500 steps in the ten minutes he's allowed there after his shower. The emptiness isn't something he wants to stow inside; but any sudden commotion jerks the feeling back. Only when he's being interrogated does he feel whole. The questions and the fear of beatings permeate his body and concentrate all the loose fibers of his being into one, compressing his strength and all the time into it as well. Every coincidence, every ambiguity gives way as they press him about who he is and who he was and check all the answers against one another and throw them back at him. Tourist or terrorist, true or false, hot or cold—the emptiness has no chance to creep up. His body has weight. It's only afterward when they leave him back in his cage that there's nobody left to say I, I Rashid, a weak bundle of nerves and letters.

And once again Islam hasn't come. Islam has not come. The sentence grates inside his skull. The letters written in toothpaste flicker in front of his eyes. His hands prickle and his shoulders cramp but he's got to stay still. He can't lose his patience. Kirat is shy. The murmuring may be scaring the lizard off. Maybe it's not used to its name yet. The *chaplain* used to have another name, an American name, before he became a *chaplain*. Then he converted to Islam and was renamed Mohammad Halabi-Islam. He had told Rashid about the imam in Damascus who had given him the name. Damascus is huge. It's the bride of the Levant, the oldest city in the world. You have to turn to the south there to pray. The imam is a Muslim pastor who helps show people the way. Allah has many names. Mohammad had showed Rashid the chapter. *Allah is He, than Whom there is no other god—The Sovereign, the Holy One; The Source of Peace and Perfection. He is Allah, the Creator, The Evolver, The Bestower of Forms. To Him belong The Most Beautiful Names.* There are exactly ninety-nine names, Mohammad says. But you're also allowed to pick one out yourself. It's no different than with the lizard. The most important thing is that you think on Allah. It's difficult for Rashid to think on Allah. He has the voice of a loudspeaker, but no appearance. The lizard doesn't even have a voice. It's as far away as Allah. The entire prison camp is full of shapes that don't exist. Murmurs come from all around, like the light crisscrossed on the ground, the light that makes his orange suit look violet. Once again Islam hasn't come. Rashid sits up. He kneels on the ground, leans forward over the toothpaste writing with his hands palm down like an orange praying. His back hurts. The shadow of his body overtakes the latticed shadows on the ground. *Cleared by U.S. Forces.* The chalky scribble of K-I-R-A-T is all that's left, an empty message. Nobody around. No Kirat. He rubs his hands over the toothpaste until the letters are gone.

His hands are covered with sticky dust. He puts them on either side of the ground he's wiped and bends all the way forward. Here on the ground is where he belongs. They're never going to let him go. He hears voices around him. His cheek touches the ground. Viscous fluid pools in his nostrils. He sniffs and the stuff is sucked down his throat into the emptiness, into his hollowed out innards. He closes his eyes and listens to the murmurs and laughs. They are behind him, over him. He doesn't want to see them—he knows they're talking about him even if they are doing it secretly, in a coded language. The high-pitched, childish voices are artificially hushed. Sometimes they are so soft all you hear is a paper-like whisper, knowing and spiteful. School children, healthy and happy and on the right side; they lean together in the corner and look over their shoulders: *Evil is the home of the wrongdoers! Soon will ye be vanquished and gathered together to Hell—an evil bed indeed to lie in. Taste ye the Penalty of the Scorching Fire!* Snickers emerge from the whispers. Engulfed. Chalk lines on enclosed asphalt, heaven and hell. *Nothing cool shall they taste therein, nor any drink save a boiling fluid.* Prostrated on the floor with their asses in the air and their arms stretched out in front of them, laughing at the non-believers. *They will be Companions of the Fire—dwelling therein forever.*

An evil bed. He's not a wrong doer. But despite that this is an evil bed. There's no fire, but it does burn. Water doesn't help. He had thrown cold water on the ground and prayed naked on the bare floor. Get me out of here. His knees hurt. Ninety-nine names and not one of them is right. *Baba.* Get me out of here. The fence is too high. The chalk square is too small. Only his feet fit in it if he positions them right. Each foot directly next to the other. Leave me alone. They peer at his bare feet sticking out from under his behind. When they whisper he doesn't move. He just stays on the floor. He prays. The throng he hears behind him begins to thin, the voices scatter. There are a few last scraping sounds, then echoes. The path is empty. There's just a dim sound left now, the sustained notes of "A" and "I," "A" and "I." He prays toward the plywood wall, facing north, facing home, *la ilaha illa -'llah*, "A" and "I"—it's Rashid, I'm here. He clenches his hands into fists and puts his head to the floor. The sound is familiar, a gentle old voice. He tries to hold onto the voice. "A" and "I"—*habib*, darling, kiddie, I, Rashid, Gandhi. It comes in so many forms. He's not alone. *Habib, bacha tumhara baba.* His *Nani* sits near him with her back to him; she's squatting on her heels with her prayer beads in her hand. Crosshatched pattern on the ground. Street noises outside. She's so close by, praying peacefully, stringing the prayers along in the obscure vibrato of Urdu: *Habib, bacha tumhara bap.* She's old. She knows everything. She knows him. You're just a boy, a tourist. *Adab, Nani.* I've come to visit you. I don't speak any Urdu. She keeps counting off the prayer beads. Murmuring. *Habib, bacha walid ka.* He lets himself be lulled by the sounds. Then noise and heat all around—artificial daylight filled with people, motion, glinting and glaring, cage doors rattling, changing of the guard. He crouches on his knees, trying to compact himself into the smallest amount of space, trying to stay within the boundaries of the smeared chalk lines. He tries to wrap himself in the protective sound of Urdu murmurs. He squeezes his eyes shut.

The half-darkness is strange and stuffy. The old lady scurries meekly around the room. Her murmurs have become mumbles, and the sound is Pashtuni. She doesn't look at him. *A 's-salamu alaykum, Ana.* She's afraid of him. He's a visiting fighter, a man among many men. They all lay in sleeping bags on the bare floor, all hiding in the darkness. The *Ana* is the only one up, mumbling to herself. She doesn't trust him. The noises outside are the sound of war-shouts and fists and blood and punches—and the prayers do no good. The noise of battle comes nearer and drowns out the *Ana's* voice. Someone throws open the windows and doors and the sudden glare blinds Rashid. The light rushes into his eyes. The enemy enters with heavy steps, weapons rattling. His shadow blots out the light and he screams: *Shut up!* There's a greenish gray smear on the floor.

The Uzbek punches on the chain link fence. *Come on, man.* A new MP, blond, is standing in the flood-light in front of the next cage down. He sticks out his chin, betraying his fear of this raging, wild animal in the stall. Another guard, tall, appears behind him, bored, relaxed, arms crossed, barely listening to what's going on; he looks over his shoulder as the small, dark figure of the doctor approaches along the path. *No trips to the latrine after sunset*, says the new MP as he takes a step closer to the pris-oner. The tall one steps closer, too, and Rashid catches the glint of eyeglasses—it's him, *time to strip* MP. Rashid slumps from his knees onto his side on the mattress, covering his face with his arms. His skin moist and guts quivering, he doesn't want another look at that face. He pictures him baring his teeth as he hears the familiar voice: *If you don't stop*, he snarls, *I'll chain you up for the rest of the fucking night.* There's a third voice now, cheerful and chummy: *Those are the only kind of words these animals understand.* There's a throat-clearing noise above Rashid's head—it sounds like it's right in his cage. He pulls aside his arm but doesn't lift his head. The doctor is clucking his tongue. He's standing right out front of Rashid's cage, and as Rashid moves his arms aside the doctor glances sideway at him and looks Rashid right in the eyes. It's quiet. *Please*, Rashid whispers—or at least thinks, though what comes out of his mouth is a strange, barely-audible, whistling sound. The doctor is hunched over and looks sad. The light shows deep creases in his sallow face. He doesn't react. Not even his eyes move. Beyond him the shapes of the other two soldiers shift slowly across Rashid's field of view. The MP with glasses is blocked from view by the doctor's body. Rashid folds his hands together and places them in his lap and pulls his legs tightly together. He can hear the crunch of the steps of the MP with glasses between the doctor and the tall MP with the pockmarked face. The walkie-talkie crackles. The shape of four-eyes-MP reappears from behind the doctor's silhouette, bursting Rashid's fantasy that he's no longer there. The MP retreats down the path a few steps and disappears. Rashid lifts his head and sits upright. The doctor's shadow slants across the glowing white sheet and the right side of Rashid's hips—right where the doctor has stuck him with needles while holding him with his thick but gentle hands. Somewhere out of view the walkie-talkie crackles and beeps like an alarm. *I want to know,* Rashid says quickly, his voice sounding hollow and old, rasping in his throat. *Please. When do you think I can go home?*

The doctor's body suddenly shudders and tenses as if Rashid has startled him in the middle of a deep thought. He exhales loudly, an impatient sigh that dissolves into a word: *Home.* He's silent. Rashid is silent. All the voices well up, chanting *Ask your interrogators,* a spiteful chorus: *Ask your interrogators, ask your interrogators.* He's afraid they'll drown out the doctor's answer. *Home,* the doctor repeats. *All of us wanna go home.* He takes a step back and turns to face Rashid, his body small, fleshy, awash in light. *Okay,* he says, *listen.* More static from the walkie-talkie. The doctor speaks slowly, very slowly, and emphasizes each word: *I don't talk about when you're going home, and just because you're here doesn't mean it will be soon.* Rashid's heart beats and he counts the seconds as the words percolate through him, calming words, one after the other until the last one, *soon.* A wave builds in his chest, washes upwards and waits to recede. The tension continues. The doctor's face is lit up like the moon above the sea, round and cold, and a shiver runs over the surface. At that same moment he notices the young, blond soldier—the new guy—waiting for the doctor a few yards down the path. *Ask your interrogator,* the doctor says and turns away. His boots crunch on the gravel. He doesn't look back. Only the MP turns back and looks at Rashid with the white, familiar face of a child.

Then the coast is clear. Empty. Everything happens very quickly, unstoppable and violent. A silent explosion. *Home.* His body cavity contracts. Rashid jerks his shoulders up and tries to stay still. Shirt and pants on his body. The material gives off a violet glow, dull gray in recesses where it's wrinkled. The distinct meshed grids of shadows cover the dull concrete floor. Creeping sensations on his feet. Two feet next to each other on the concrete. Waves roar in Rashid's ears, phantom waves, waves of pressure. The waste bucket, newly disinfected, glows white in the corner. Behind it is a pile of stuff—dish towel, liquid soap, the Koran, the water flask, toothpaste, everything's there as always. The large towel is hanging in a bundle from the fence on the opposite side. The small towel is balled up on the mattress, with light on it. The fence and gate facing the path seem very close. They always seem to be getting closer. The steel rods and chain link fencing glitter in the floodlights, and on the other side of the path light glints off the metal beams of those cages, as well. And the outfits of the prisoners over there look purple, too. Their towels and buckets give off a white glow. Reality closes in on him from all sides and soon it will slam against him. There's no way out. The water bucket filled with water, cool water, early morning cool, early morning the muezzin, breakfast, the water warms up, tomorrow afternoon a shower and a trip to the recreation area. Tomorrow. Tomorrow everything loosens up. The noise is insufferable. Rashid tries to block it out, sits still like everything around him. He's silent, as if he doesn't exist. Silent, as if nothing around him exists, either. His blood boils, pulsing loudly in his ears. His breathing gets slow and shallow. His heart and lungs are calm while the commotion around him rises and falls. He looks around and sees his own hunched shadow plastered to the plywood wall. Just like every night. Just like the lizard that time.

He stands up. Nothing has happened, but the emptiness inside him has expanded, nothingness taking over his entire body—limbs now just empty pipes made of skin and muscle. It feels artificial, floating in space, nothing inside him to weight him down. Stiffly he takes the two steps to the front wall, shaky on his feet. It's as if he fills the cage, expanding like seeping gas, nearly reaching the ceiling that here on the path side of the cage is several feet above his head. He's unsteady, not sure what to do with his empty body. Mosquitoes flit above the water bucket. The surface of the water has a white luminescence. He sticks his pointer finger in, just the tip, and breaks through the glowing surface. It's cool and wet, nothing more. He has to conserve this carefree feeling of nothingness. He lets his arms dangle and watches as a drop of water falls from his finger. It falls through the lines of shadow and light. He's forgotten what real darkness is like. He can't see the floodlights—they are installed on poles high above the paths. When you look up it feels as if salt is being strewn from above, burning and blinding your eyes. But you can sense the darkness even farther up, above the floodlights. The lights don't shine on anything specific, just the tops of the cages and empty roofs. To his right the Uzbek lies there curled up like a baby on his mattress, his behind hanging over the edge. He's wrapped his arms around his face and put a washcloth over his feet. No patrols. It's quiet—either that or Rashid's gone deaf. With his wet finger he traces the wire frame of one of the links in the fence and then lets his finger glide downward along the wire honeycomb. His finger hops from the inside of one opening to the next. He doesn't want to bend down and is careful not to squander his feeling of weightlessness. Suddenly something happens, a barely visible movement on the other side of the path. A prisoner on the other side, standing like Rashid inside four walls, right against the front wall of his cage, raises his hand. Maybe he's just trying to shield his eyes from the floodlights. But there he is, looking out with his hand held up. Rashid raises his hand, waits, and then lets his hand fall again. There's a pause, then the other prisoner lets his hand drop, too; it's like a distant, time-delayed mirror image. The orange turns and disappears into the depth of his cage. It's over. The path is lit up and empty. A car sputters. A dog yaps, stops, and yaps again. Somewhere over by the watchtower a soldier barks out something that sounds like an answer. The Uzbek growls, stretches out his legs, and begins to mumble. Rashid turns around: behind him the cage. The cage has been expecting him.

There's only one step in one direction, right into the middle. A second would lead to the other wall. He can't step backwards at all, as he's already against the front wall. There's only one thing he can do, the usual. As if there's another way, or someplace to take a break. His sheets glow beneath the lattice of shadows. When he lies down that same grate will enclose him and he'll just wait for some sort of numbness to take hold. Kirat is gone. Kirat had never been there—it was just a row of letters written in reverse order. The *chaplain* is gone, Muhammad or James, the cleric with all his names; maybe he's taken Allah, all 99, with him back to Damascus and forgotten all about Rashid. There's nobody here anymore. Everything's gone, and all clues of their existence have been erased. The cage is empty. His body is empty. *Ask your interrogators—* question the questioners. A question mark that curves back on itself, a never-ending loop in which the questions answer themselves until all answers have become questions. *Ask your interrogators.* The providers of answers are gone, and there's no one left to ask. There's nobody around. He can't even talk to himself anymore—all that's left is an empty husk that breathes and beats inside. He's already mute. Now he wishes he were deaf, as well.

Slowly so as not to startle himself, he takes three tiny steps from the front wall into the cage. Standing on the balls of his feet, he shudders thinking about touching the mattress. It sits there full of debris, shards and drizzles, all the stuff that's been carved out of him—the spasms and pain that make him twitch. But he's got nothing left and it's just one step away; he lets himself flop onto the sweat-soaked cloth, onto the lumpy, wrinkled rectangle where he spends every night trying to watch over his dead-tired body. Every night with voices in his head and a hole in his guts, a hole carved out by endless questions. He doesn't want it all to come back. Maybe he can just play dead. But it waits for him under his eyelids, beyond which it's never dark. Against a smeared concrete-gray background is the same perpetual image: Rashid, on his back, his musty body a splotch wrapped in orange clothes and moist skin. The gray expanse bakes, sizzling and smoking in his ears, and outside he hears a loud crackling. He rubs his eyes with his fists, pushing deep into the spongy brain matter in an effort to banish the image of the Uzbek standing in the corner and aiming into the waste bucket. The blurred images twinkle and flit, mix together. You have to press in just the right spot to burst them. And still they slip away and squirt out to the edges, disappear, reappear somewhere else. He winces and rubs harder. Colors appear. Bursts of yellow remind him of the speckles on Kirat's back; the colors shift and transform like the lizard's skin. Voices: *Allahu akbar, Mr. Bakhrani we need your help, in the name of Allah, the most merciful, please answer, read the last suras, answer precisely, get back in your fucking cage, it all depends on you, habib, bacha tumhara baba, be calm, ask your interrogators, O Prophet rouse the Believers to the fight.* He lets his hands drop from his eyes and blinks in the pale light until the flickering images stop. The voices continue to whisper incomprehensibly.

Rashid looks at his legs, able to see the thighs ending in his knees like stumps, the rest of each leg cut off from view. Somewhere out of view it itches. He rolls his head to the side, now able to see a bare foot. He needs to scratch it, but can't muster the strength—doesn't want to. He wants nothing to do with any of it. Nothing to do with the itching, nothing to do with the urge to stand up and piss in the bucket. It's his right foot, the one with calluses forming over the old scar. He can make the foot disappear without moving—all he has to do is shift his eyes slightly. They dilate as they focus on the water bucket which is very close by. Then the chain links behind it come into view, and the path and cages beyond. Then his eyes light on his foot again, chafed and swollen, as both feet are. Dizziness spreads from behind his eye and becomes a mild headache. The itching begins to radiate out as well, shimmering like something between foreground and background, between the world outside and the surface of the eye. A no man's land. Blades of grass grow there, dry and rough—the kind of grass that pricks at the bottom of your feet and catches at your ankles when you run through it barefoot. Joints flexing, heels bouncing, the hard, dry ground beneath your feet races backwards. The sky races backwards, too, but the horizon continues to move away with every stride. Grass and air alternating underfoot, sky and ground, feet floating above and then stabbing into the dirt. In midair a figure pops out of the grass, something dark amidst the golden waves of grass. It waves, yells something, disturbing but alluring. The horizon stops receding, legs pump in the air. Who is it? He's descending back to earth. Just before the impact, the answer. But then he's on his back again, his eyes focused close rather than in the distance, his knees in view. He can still hear the call: Rashid. But the name of the other person is gone. It's a dream. A dream from an earlier time. He doesn't want to let it get away, wants to reenter the dream, run, find the answer, *the names. It all depends on you.* He tries to prop himself up but all he feels is the softness beneath him, the sheets beneath his feet. *Just because you're here doesn't mean it will be soon.* His legs cramp up. He opens his mouth wide and presses his tongue into his gums to try to hold down the scream that wells up in his chest. He closes his eyes and stares into the great wide nothingness, wrapped in orange cloth that glows violet in this light. It's a bottomless pit, frayed at the edges like a sore and swallowing everything that falls in: light, wire, visions, kicks and punches, voices, noises and orders and prayers and questions and whispers—but nothing concrete, no stories or names or answers.

He falls into this depthless spring, falling and falling, until he hears the voice again, the one he can't really make out: Rashid, it says, raspy and raw, Rashid Bakhrani, "A" and "I," "A" and "I." It entwines him like rope, calling *la ilaha illa - 'llah* as if coming from a loudspeaker far, far away, somewhere up above, outside the blazing red dome of the bottomless pit. The walls absorb the sound, but Rashid hears every word. Question the questioner, says the voice in Arabic. Rashid understands— it's the voice from Damascus and he hasn't been forgotten. They know what's happened to him. They're talking about what's happened to him. I can't stand up, Rashid says. It all depends on you, says the voice, you just have to talk. I can't talk, Rashid says. The imam is silent. He wants to show him the way, without a blindfold: Look toward Mecca, toward the watchtower, past the paved recreation space and on toward the interrogators' barracks. It's time. Just give them the right answers. To obey the voice he would have to move, but if he moves the voice disappears. How can he follow the advice? Rashid keeps his eyes closed and listens. Now it's coming from very close by, crackling, its thin reverberations fading into the depths, echoing down the dark, narrow streets of a giant city. Is Allah not the most righteous and wise judge? Just tell everything, say who you are and what you've done. The imam leads him along, takes him to pray. Rashid knows the last suras, *they are short.* He's ready. *Verily the Day of Sorting Out is a thing appointed. The Day that The Spirit and the angels will stand forth in ranks, None shall speak except any who is permitted by Allah Most Gracious, and he will say what is right.* I'm a believer, says Rashid, speaking in Arabic, the language of prayer. The Jama Masjid mosque was right near *Nani's* place. I went there often. Out of the stench and bustle of Old Delhi, shoes left outside, peering out of the courtyard at the sky and the sun above the smog. I knew Allah was there. And all the men thought I was one of them. Muhammad went to Damascus; I went to Delhi. As soon as I have my shop, I'll be a Muslim. I already know the prayers by heart.

Rashid waits, his eyes closed tightly to avoid looking into the glaring interrogation lamps. The low parts of the city glitter, reddish sweat oozing from every pore, the walls of the fort gleaming like meat at the market. *And what will explain to thee what Hell-Fire is?* It's silent. The orange shirt sticks to Rashid's skin in the heat. His back hurts, but he doesn't dare move. A crackle as the imam clears his throat. Rashid senses the imam nodding his head and smiling. I believe you, he says in Arabic, smiling. Rashid remembers he wanted to ask a question, a question about the shop and the money he got from his grandmother to cover the deposit and rent and set up and delivery van and labor. *Ask your interrogators.* But he can't remember what he wanted to ask. And he can't speak except about what is right. He needs to prove he's a warrior. *Those who believe, and fight for the Faith, in the cause of Allah, as well as those who give them asylum and aid—these are all in very truth the Believers: For them is the forgiveness of sins and a provision most generous. And those who accept Faith subsequently, and fight for the Faith in your company—they are of you.* We split up the guard duties, Rashid says. I slept in the garage twice—once with Massoud and once with Hamid—to make sure nobody stole the truck. We built a secret drawer under the bed of the truck where we were going to hide things from the border guards. Hamid's father fought against the Russians with the mujahideen. Now the Americans were there. The war was still going, and I was there.

Rashid's knees are shaking. His tongue is dry. There's water right there. But it's impossible to loosen his muscles and stand up. He lets his head loll to the side. His skull cap arches over his head, tall like the dome inside the approaching train station, dim and full of echoes. The scent of fruit and vegetables is in the air, and a palette of flowers is whisked past by a forklift leaving its sweetness trailing behind. It's Monday, the wholesale market day, paradise. *The sincere and devoted servants of Allah—for them is a Sustenance determined, fruits; and they shall enjoy honor and dignity, in Gardens of Felicity, facing each other on Thrones of dignity: Round will be passed to them a Cup from a clear-flowing fountain—*that's just a fairytale. He need only stretch out his hand to touch the roses. Flower sellers are standing in line and Mehmet waves hello above the crowd. Rashid turns toward him. The imam places his cool hands on Rashid's temples; no, it's not the imam—it's a breeze against his warm face. But something is touching him. And he smells perfumed shampoo and wet wool on cold fingers. There's a face, too, the face he had tried to remember in the shower stall, with blond ringlets tickling the forehead and falling over the ears. The ears are small with silver earrings in them, they peek out from under a blue hat. Hair, curls, ears, while Mehmet waves the bunch of roses. Mehmet. Jenny: a name out of a dream about a fair face, a fair hand in his hand, leading him toward the door. The door opens and the light from inside falls across the snow. It smells like fresh laundry. He knows this dream, snow and roses and earrings and forklifts, it's all there—and they are waiting for an answer: *When do you think I can go home?* They follow him and protect him, they always find him again, even here in the depths of hell in Damascus. *For the Rejecters We have prepared Chains, Yokes, and a Blazing Fire. Soon will I cast them into Hell-Fire! Naught doth it permit to endure, and naught doth it leave alone. Darkening and changing the color of man. With Us are Fetters to bind them, and a Fire to burn them, and a Food that chokes, and a Penalty Grievous. A 's-salamu alaykum,* says the imam, reading the short sura. Say who you were, ask your questions, take the names, spit them out. Then it's finally over and Rashid lifts his head and opens his eyes. He puts his hands on the mattress and sits up. Mama, he says loudly. His tongue pulls away from his gums and his gullet rasps. Jenny, he says. Cute little silver lizards cling to her earlobes. Mehmet, he says. With every utterance the emptiness inside him starts to fill. It feels good to blurt it out. *Baba.* It helps bind the gaping wound in his heart and suture closed the rifts the emptiness has opened. It's nighttime. It's bright out. Rashid sits in his cage and his shadow falls across the sheet.

He grabs the balled up towel, shakes it out, and places it on his head. It's so easy to turn it into a turban and secure it. He tucks the corner under the rolled edge and he's wearing a magic hat. His Uzbek neighbor snores; he's lying on his back with his arms under the back of his head and his mouth open. His feet are covered with one washcloth, another one is next to his head. Rashid has never heard his name. He stands up; the hole in his innards is gone and everything feels compact and dense inside, even full. He kneels down next to the waste bucket, opens his pants and pisses quietly, aiming the stream against the side of the bucket and enjoying the feeling of it flowing out. His shadow looms against the plywood wall surrounded by the latticed shadows of the fencing. He leans toward the wall and the outline of his shadow sharpens. His nose, chin and forehead touch the fence and he presses his face against it. His cheeks and lips give against the mesh, and he touches the warm, hard wire with his tongue. The turban shifts and he reaches up and removes it. He puts the towel over the top of the waste bucket. Then he organizes the little things next to it. He puts the prayer cap, toothpaste, toothbrush, liquid soap and shampoo bottle on the dishtowel and then puts another washcloth on top of it all. He puts the Koran on the mattress.

He unscrews the top of the water flask and walks to the front of the cage and dunks it in the water bucket. Drinks. Sits down on the mattress again. Throws open the book nearly to the last page. *In the name of Allah, the Most Merciful.* Sura 93. *By the Glorious Morning Light, and by the Night when it is still.* Words he knows by heart, like the words in the letters: My dear Rashid, we are always with you. We are doing all we can to get you home. Then four lines are redacted with black bars. *Thy Guardian-Lord hath not forsaken thee, nor is He displeased.* You'll just have to hang on until then. *Verily the hereafter will be better for thee than the present.* Just do what they ask of you, *And soon will thy Guardian-Lord give thee that wherewith thou shalt be well-pleased.* Two more lines blotted out with black bars. Don't give up. I am sure we will see you again soon. Your *Baba. Cleared by U.S. Forces.* Rashid lifts the flask to his mouth. *Did He not find thee an orphan and give thee shelter and care?* The water's lukewarm and tastes like rubber and chlorine. But he drinks every drop. *Did he not find thee wandering and give thee guidance?* He slams the Koran shut and tosses the flask onto the mattress. *He found thee in need, and made thee independent.*

Beyond the two empty cages on one side nothing is moving. The Uzbek on the other side sleeps. It's all peaceful in the cages on the other side of the path. The path itself is empty. Even so Rashid yanks the blue plastic blanket from between the mattress and the fence and lays it at the head of the bed. Then he reaches under it and grabs the corner of the sheet and tries with both hands to rip it until the material gives. The sharp ripping—clean and straight, fiber after fiber—sounds like music, getting higher and higher. Rashid feels a strange, liberating sense of relaxation in his face, lifting his spirits: You see, Kirat, he laughs, how easy it is, and on the rest they may print their flag. He rips one last bit and out pops a white strip from under the blue tarp. It's something new, something homemade. At this exact moment the snoring in the adjoining cage abruptly stops. Rashid jumps and looks up. He is looking into a wide open pair of eyes. Without averting his eyes, the Uzbek rolls to the side, props himself up, noisily guzzles some water, clears the phlegm in his throat, spits in the bucket, and then looks away. *Schleep*, he says. *Josch*. He rubs his eyes with his knuckles and then braces his fists on the mattress to help himself slowly stand up. He looks down at Rashid silently. He spits in the bucket again then steps up to the fence closest to Rashid's cage. He points to his chest and says *man*. Then he says something else: *Ot-tis-olte*. As he says this he holds up both hands with all his fingers splayed out, closes and reopens them two more times, then holds up his left hand open and the right closed except for his thumb: thirty-six. Then he points at Rashid. *You?*

Rashid looks at the welts on the Uzbek's wrists and then at his own fist, which grips the end of the white strip of cloth, shaking. His whole body is shaking, pulsing with life and shaking with rage as if he were freezing cold—even as sweat drips down his neck to his chest, pooling in the indentations between his ribs. He lifts up the tarp and sticks his fist under it, stashing the strip of cloth. Talk, pass the time, lost time, time in the cage. He doesn't want to think about how old he is. Four hands' worth when he got here. He looks at his feet. In this light the red sores on his ankles look bluish, and the skin around his toenails is torn and frayed. *Josch*. The Uzbek waves his right hand to get Rashid's attention and points to his own chest again. *Man*, he says, *Sadik*. "A" and "I." Sadik and Tarik—it never ends. *You*, he says, pointing at Rashid. He puts his arms out to his sides, shrugs his shoulders and raises his eyebrows quizzically. Rashid, says Rashid, nodding. Rashid, repeats the Uzbek. Rashid holds up two open hands, closes them and opens them again: *twenty*, he says. *Twenty*, the Uzbek repeats. Shadow grids on his feet, his pants, the sheet. They'll never give him another sheet when they see what he's done to this one. And there's no place to hide the strip he's ripped off. *Sleep!* He blurts it out loudly, leaning his head to one side and slamming the palms of his hands into the fence. *Schleep*, repeats the Uzbek, nodding slowly. His shadow extends out from the floor of his cage. *You look*, he says, and turns his back to Rashid. He lifts his shirt up. A raised black scar extends from midway down his back up to his shoulder blade. Looking over his shoulder, his slanted eyes gleam, squinting. Sadik lets his shirt down and turns back toward Rashid. He points to himself. *Man*, he says. Then gestures to his wound: *no schleep*. He wags his finger in warning and then lets himself drop heavily to his mattress. He curls up with his back to Rashid. Rashid stares at the Uzbek's violet shirt and traces the hidden scar in his mind. His eyes wander down across the seat of his pants to his covered legs and his bare feet. Rashid's sweating and fidgeting. Suddenly Sadik turns over and reaches for the towels. The larger one he spreads out over his feet. The small one he puts over his face. Then he curls back up. He throws his upper body around restlessly. *Sadik no schleep, Rashid no schleep, Sadik no schleep, no schleep, no schleep.* The little washcloth on his face puffs up and down as he babbles.

The prison lives, silently, abandoned. Now the only commotion is beneath Rashid's skin. Sudden surges. His jugular throbs against his collar and his heartbeat pounds in his ears. Sleep. Sleep in the safety of the cage. But suddenly the walls seem so far away that his body wants to race over and touch them. What Rashid would really like to do is cling to the Uzbek three steps away, curl up, hold on, share the sensation of his breathing and heart beat. Or wake him up, beat on the fence, Sadik, Tarik, *no schleep*; kill the time and the endlessly expanded space. But Sadik's dismissed him. Now Rashid has to wait. He sits on his mattress but can't lie down and snuggle the blue blanket—his sheet's ruined. Under the tarp is the strip of cloth. Sadik's mumbling has become rhythmic and faint. Every third or fourth breath the tone rises a little; he's far away, somewhere in Uzbekistan or Afghanistan, envisioning battles, wounds, scars. *You*, Rashid. His name is back. It bumbles its way into a distant dream and now the name pulses through Rashid's own ears and deep into his brain, where his memories reside—memories of something heavy, round and complete, like sleep as he once knew it. Sleeping from exhaustion, abandoning yourself and completely shutting down, because you're at the end of your rope. And then to wake up. *No, no schleep.* Don't lie down, don't wait, don't listen to the latest noises filling the empty space with clicks and whooshes and rattles. The emptiness is now on the outside, in the cage, in the light, all around, and he feels like a tiny speck in a dizzying wide-open space. There's nobody to keep him from disappearing in it. He thinks about Kirat, about the resistance of the fabric of the sheet, and about that moment of happiness when it began to rip. He reaches for the tarp. He feels the balled up cloth band through the smooth plastic. Just at that moment he's violently shaken: He's catapulted at incredible speed into the emptiness, a bullet hurtling toward a frontier marked by a black wall of nothingness. The speed compresses the air in his lungs and tears him open. Everything races backwards; everything is behind him. The only thing holding him is the strip of cloth, the last shred, ripping and screeching, music in a silent storm.

Rashid catches his breath as steps approach. He's cold. His clenched jaw hurts. Quick, hard steps. They're coming—with the dog—like they always do at night. They'll walk past, or stop in front of a cage and shake the fence and yell. The dog will bark; maybe it can smell the cold fear in his sweat. They're always walking around, listening, watching, sniffing. The night is short. Rashid lets himself fall to his side without taking his hand from the tarp. He clutches the strip of cloth, the last shred. He won't let go of it and nobody will separate him from it. Another six or seven steps and their shadows will jut across the concrete floor. He needs a bucket. The water bucket is full. There's no way he can pour it all out. He listens, peeks out of half-closed eyes, and suppresses his agitated breathing. Carefully in and out he breathes. He's pissed in the waste bucket. He'll have to use that one. He can dump it out at the back of the cage, toward the plywood wall. Sadik has stopped mumbling; he must have fallen asleep. They're almost to his cage. Rashid closes his eyes all the way. He hears the dog panting. His own breathing picks up, louder and quicker—easy now, easy. He'll dump the piss out of the water bucket. He doesn't want anything to attract attention. They pass. Finally. One is talking. It's the freckled MP. *Married*, Rashid hears, *September*. It'll be a while before they come back around. He lifts his head. The two of them are walking down the middle of the path. One is holding the leash but the German shepherd is already out of sight. They disappear. His fear disappears. They're in a hurry. He's in a hurry.

He sits up. Sadik has taken the towel off his head, but he's covered his face again with his arm as if to signal to Rashid that he won't interfere. Rashid gets up from the mattress. It won't be easy, he thinks, and a strange smirk spreads across his face again: he's never hanged himself before. He gets to work. He's efficient but quiet. Again he feels satisfied at the magic that everything has a point, a place. He dumps the urine into the water and flips the waste bucket over. Finally he's able to move about freely. He steps onto the bucket; his head touches the top of the cage. He steps off again and coils the strip of cloth. It's narrow and strong, good. It's short—ripped from one of the short sides of the sheet. He sizes it up against the wall, calculating: half the length minus the circumference of his neck has to be shorter than the height of the bucket. He'll need a little extra for the knots. There's enough, but it's going to be difficult to keep his body from reaching the ground. He'll have to stand on his toes to tie the noose as close to the roof crossbeam as possible. He can use the Koran, too, and the washcloth. His desire is making him resourceful. Ever so often he looks up. Outside it's like a silent, glowing stage covered with thousands of spider webs, and sometimes a violet puppet moves within the nest of shadows. Then he pictures himself fumbling about, a violet clown with his head bent down in front of a tower made of towels and a bucket with a book on top of it. He has a loop tied around his neck, eager and focused on his task as if his life depends on it. With the noose hanging down his back, he claws at the chain link fencing to brace himself as he climbs onto the shaky structure. He wobbles and even without standing on his toes his head is already bent forward because it's against the top of the cage. He passes the noose over the crossbeam and shifts onto the balls of his feet. Luckily his moist feet stick to the cover of the Koran giving him traction. Passing the cloth from one hand to the other, he wraps it a couple times around the beam and pulls the ends and ties them to each other. There's nothing left, just wheezing and sweating, dangling cloth ends and the hidden noose and the wobbling underfoot. The knots need to be strong but still have give at the neck, not too much, not too little. There has to be enough length to fall and swing, but not enough to reach the ground. His arms are limp. His feet maintain balance. He tests the knots, letting his neck pull against the noose. Now the noose is taut, but not too tight, and he lets go, no hands, finally free.

Beneath him is a whole new cage, suddenly huge, the floor far below his outstretched feet, and between, all that still holds him. Then suddenly he's afraid he won't be able to get off the creative tower he's built—he thought more about how to get high enough than how to fall back down. But nothing's going to remedy that now. It'll have to do. He'll just have to kick the book and bucket out from under himself and lift his legs. Just don't catch yourself, don't use your hands. He stands on his toes and tries to figure out the right motion, the right command to send his muscles. He looks at his rubber sandals, black and white, Chinese flip-flops. That's what they're called, and the toe-piece rubs the sand between the toes on the way to the water, *Baba*'s camera behind him. His browned child, carrying a red bucket, is naked except for his flip-flops. The right foot hovers at the edge of the turquoise surface extending out to the horizon. The foot quivers above the tiny waves—just one more step and the bliss will speed through his limbs. He breaks through the surface with a dull thud, a dog howls, his head snaps back and his eyes jerk open. Finally darkness.

Schleep. No schleep. Floating. Far below the floor and the deathless murmuring and an olive green rectangle getting smaller and smaller. There lies Rashid, tiny. Sleeping, swaying, floating, up in the night sky where the cold lamp of the moon hangs, doughy yellow with dark valleys. *Home.* Slowly he descends and the murmuring continues. That's the doctor. That's the stretcher. That's the infirmary. That's English: *no problem, we'll handle it as usual, and then Zoloft once a day.* He feels the injection, *Zoloft, Zoloft.* He's sick, he's dying, and the imam leans over him looking sad. His eyes gleam above his big nose, and his beard shakes. He too speaks English: *I trust you, you're free, you're my man, you're free.*

V. *Jihad.* Dreaming

The numbness slowly fades. Rashid doesn't move. He is silent, hidden in his skin, feeling his pores open. It's like waking up, though he knows he's been lying here for a while, contorted, on his side, his arms and face smashed into the floor. The surface beneath him has gotten harder. Ha rd and granular like asphalt. He can feel it scraping and cutting into his cheek, and at the same time a wild premonition.

His heart begins to beat again and jolts him back to life. The thick blanket of silence enveloping him dissolves into thin air—sticky air, drenched in dense gases and smells, heavy and warm. But something is protecting him from the sun. He remembers that he hadn't hung a towel on the fence. He carefully opens his eyes. Very nearby—only a few inches away—is a strange sight: a gouged, weather-beaten wall. Something is filtering the light from above, an awning or an umbrella. Jumpy shadows twitch in the reddish light. They jerk across the crumbling surface of the wall, gravelly cement patched with pink plaster. It's a wall you'd only see outside. It's spray-painted with black hooks and dots, and covered with stiff, cracked pieces of paper. Beneath the rolled top edge a melted, washed out face of a woman with black eyebrows and lips stares out blankly. She's unaffected by the light flickering in her eyes. Rashid turns his head to try to figure out what's casting the shadows. They flow into one another, gliding across the dust-colored floor and the mottled, light cloth—a sheet or shirt—draped over him. He sees now the shadows have feet. The feet walk right over his face, rising before his eyes to reveal the checkered soles, bare feet and feet in rubber flip-flops with the strap between the big toe and the other four. It's the feet of prisoners. They swarm on the path, dirty street feet. Some graze him, jostle him, shove him against the wall. With every blow his head jerks and his ear grinds against the floor, ceaselessly chafing and rubbing and scraping. He waits and listens. And as he seeks to isolate the crushing sound of boot steps within the whisper of countless feet, his ears pick up something else in the gauzy, muddled noise: the scream of life up there, the music of men and machines.

Awake now, wide awake, he begins to recognize himself, a bundle of scattered bones swaddled in white cloth. Fresh pain is starting to seep in. Each drop is precious and new. Without even moving, his body is pulling itself together. He can feel his dry limbs relaxing and straightening out. His skin is becoming more elastic and regaining its sensitivity. His body yearns to figure out what's going on around him, the gurgling, jostling, and pounding. The warm tarmac thuds softly beneath all the light feet. Every vibration blazes a new path through his body. It's as if he's freezing in the heat; a thousand tiny needles synchronize and begin to probe, taste and differentiate themselves. The new reality evolves in time-lapse fashion. The stinging in his sinuses is sweat, warm, pungent sweat; it pours out of the wrinkled cloth flitting before his eyes, out of the clothes and crotches above the endless sets of feet. There's another acidic smell wafting up from the ground, the stickiness of squeezed fruit—a smell similar to a market hall. He can picture the stacked pallets, crates in front of the shop, paper bags, the scale. He can smell the fruit maturing and ripening, fermenting, molding, rotting and drying up, all at once, acrid and burning. He sees the leathery peels and dried rinds crumbling into powder and dispersing, giving off an aroma like incense or Christmas—cinnamon and anise, sweet and aromatic. The smell of ether mixes with it, as well as burning rubber and diesel oil, crackling into soot. He breathes in gasoline fumes, hears firing ignitions, hissing tires, clanging metal, lead and steel. It's a filthy street. He can't stay still any longer. The whole street is rolling over and past him. They want to take him with them. Waves of noise surge toward him and break over his head. Everything frothing around him, bubbling. His body swims. The hot brine seasons and cooks his body, the motion snatches him up. He has to let himself be carried along wherever he is, whether it's in the middle of a street or out at sea. He relaxes his muscles and lifts his head. The dreamgirl on the poster looks down at him from the top of the wall and smiles. Then things rain down on him from all around: booms, firecrackers, colors, smoke. He fights for light and air, braces his feet against the wall, stretches out his arms and shouts. He yells: I'm heeeere, loud and drawn out, and again, I'm heeeere! The vowels resound like the familiar "A" and "I," "A" and "I." They fill his lungs and draw him into the world.—And the world draws him. Hands, the pressure of strong, moist hands. His own hand held by other people's hands. They stretch out his limbs, pull him from the flickering shadows, help him to his feet. No straps, no handcuffs, no leg irons. With a few swats on his back and sides they brush the dust off his shirt. They're light, friendly blows. Then the hands let go. He staggers. Nobody grabs him even though he's in the middle of the throng. There are no vice-grips on his upper arms, no hand gripping his neck. A few gleaming, black eyes greet him, peering from dark faces, then disappear behind other dark faces. He looks down at the ground, at his feet. He's able to walk by himself. They leave him alone. He takes a few steps and it's easy. Even after the second, third, and fourth steps nothing restrains him—no soldiers, no fences. One foot in front of the other he proceeds on the asphalt, his flip-flops following along with a clopping sound. Hot air drafts up his legs. The fabric of his shirt—a long tunic—dangles around his ankles. He falls in anonymously among the other tunics, white, light brown, and light blue, and the caps and turbans, the head scarves with black bands, and lets himself get pulled forward. With every move he bumps into someone else. The contact makes him flinch with fear, but he's too dazed to think or question or try to escape. He just tries to avoid falling over while pushing forward until suddenly the canopy above his head gives way to open sky and sunlight streams down over the city.

The street hurls itself at him. For one blinding second Rashid thinks the rushing wave of light will bury him or fling him back into the shadows and his dream will end there. He runs into a pole standing in the middle of all the bustle, grabs hold of it, and closes his eyes so his retinas don't burn. The heat washes down his forehead, over his shoulders and down his body. The image continues to flash on the fiery surface of his eyelids—the swarming movements, like a party on the day of his arrival. He stands at the edge with his eyes squeezed shut, a stunned bystander. He tries to make sense of this teeming vision. Everything is shaking, from the walls of buildings and columns to the metal frames of shop doorways with their rolled up security shutters to the windows above the jutting stone ledges on each floor and the shingles on the flat roofs. Rashid doesn't dare open his eyes. The vision breaks down into details—wooden doors and balconies, arcades, handrails and entranceways, air conditioners, spigots and vines, tables and chairs and water pipes, lanterns, scaffolding, chimneys and antennas, tent poles and tarps, open bags of spices, bolts of cloth, fruit stands, wooden crates, plastic containers, heaps of garbage. The entire crazy scene flaps as if being projected on a portable screen buffeted by a storm of noise. But the longer Rashid lets himself listen to the sounds with his eyes closed, the more monotonous the rhythm becomes. It spews into his ears, the fury of the fizzing waves calms down, flattens out, each one rushing and receding with the same level of noise, lapping ever more gently at his feet, softly licking the edge and then ebbing away. For a moment everything is quiet, then the noise splashes up again and the voice of a muezzin rings out.

His name wafts from on high, but the "Ah" sound in Allah branches out and bounces around in splintered echoes—like a flock of birds swooping over the roofs, flapping around looking for a place to light and sing. The city catches its breath. It feels airy, uplifting, everything hovers in the sky with the voices. It's like being on another plane somewhere between heaven and earth. The 99 names skim the city's lofty peaks, gables and battlements and tumble together into words, the choir of minarets creating a garbled shouting match, *Allahu akbar*, God is great. The tones ramble and flutter, following and repeating one another. The exultations begin to come together more and more, *ash'hadu a 'l-la ilaha illa -'llah, ash'hadu anna Muhammada 'r-rasulu 'llah*. The canopy of sound arches upward to form a huge, transparent dome, ever broader, sparkling ever more brightly, honeycombed, *hayyi 'ala 's—salah, hayyi 'ala 'l-falah*. The words separate at the highest point and then tailspin down: *hayyi 'ala 's-salah*. A few stragglers drift slowly down: *hayyi 'ala 'l-falah*. Heaven has rained down. The chorus roars anew from out of the fading tones and Rashid pops open his eyes. He knows where he is. He's standing on the side of a broad avenue. He's traveling again. He's got to get to safety. They could still pull him back. What he's looking at is no longer unfamiliar—no less familiar than Delhi or Lahore. He'll find his way. He can escape, fend for himself, save himself. He can disappear into the traffic like the calls to prayer. The imam has spoken and he has lain the city of Rashid's dreams at his feet—the mother of all cities, the earthly paradise of Damascus.

He looks at the flow of the street. On the other side, across the sidewalk, are tall, craggy facades. Their dilapidated, sand-colored surfaces have been patched and painted many times over. Beneath them is the swarming sidewalk, crushingly packed, the same as the scene behind him. The pole he's holding onto is actually the corner post of a sagging wooden arcade that shades half of the side-walk. Things at the edge of the shadow glow like the lights of a jukebox. He sets out from there. Where he'd been lying, flecks of sunlight play on colorful surfaces—a mosa-ic of cassette cases, a bright carpet, uneven rows of posters stapled up, and shifting walls of printed cloths. Nooks, hidden spaces, scenery full of shouts and laughter; drum-beats boom from a radio accompanied by smooth female vocals. Legs and rumps move between the rows of hanging goods that part just in time for heads to pass through, foreheads brushing against swirls of cloth, some of it wrapped in bunches, some stretched taut, then squinting eyes and beards appear. No camo pants. No white or black faces. No military caps. But the sense of danger still hangs over him. A tight grasp and then a dark basement, the 24-hour light of the prison camp. His path lies ahead of him, beneath the open sky. The arcades swallow up people and spit others back out, women with colorful head scarves and sinuous clerics and black-shrouded women and men in jeans and bright shirts—they all duck in and out of the sun. The flow of people in and out comes in dribbles and waves. The colorful sheets gleam, hissing at passersby, bringing them to a screeching halt, throwing up obstacles, obscuring the invisible passageways between aisles. Heads pop out of the churning surface unscathed, re-submerge, pop up again, disappear.

The warmth surges up Rashid's bare legs, and with it the desire to dive in and submerge himself. He lets go of the wooden pole and steps gingerly from the sidewalk, still bracing himself. He reaches out feet-first and hesitates to lift his head. Suddenly he feels something push against the back of his knee. Then a second time, and a third. Turning around to see what it is, he finds himself looking at the broad, wedge-shaped head of a donkey—it's been nuzzling him. Its black eyes look at him from under lids with bristly lashes and its ears fidget. The donkey's hide is the same dirty light color as Rashid's tunic. There's a leather bridle around its head and neck, and reins dangle from it. A young boy in dark clothes starts to prod the donkey from behind—he whistles at it from atop a three-wheeled fruit cart, urging the animal into the street from the curb. Rashid puts his left hand on the animal's head, between its ears. His hand sits there as if paralyzed, shocked by the soft sensation. The donkey nods; then it shakes its head to the side and Rashid looks up at the boy's childlike face as he jerks the reins. The kid looks back at him for a moment before both the animal and boy turn into the street. Bicycles ring their bells as they go past. The cart, a big wooden box with four tent poles holding up a shaky cover, lumbers and creaks. The boy smacks the donkey's hindquarters. The mangos and oranges slowly seesaw past Rashid and begin to plow their way through the crowds. Rashid grabs the side of the cart with both hands. He lets himself be pulled into the light along with the cart, wheels creaking, the tent cover providing some shade. He takes a deep breath and wades onto the steaming asphalt, looking straight ahead at the brightly lit fruit and, beyond, the donkey's perked-up ears. With every step his heart beats harder, and every breath sucks the thick steam from his lungs. By the time he finally reaches the other side of the avenue and watches the ears of the donkey fade away like two candles into a side street, his pulse races like he's climbing a cliff. He's exhausted but he's also buoyed by the rush of the city, and it's already flowing through his veins. He takes a few steps on his own.

The light flooding Rashid's eyes blinds him. The cavernous walls surrounding him swallow the street noise. There's just the clip-clop of his rubber sandals against his heels, a tiny, high-pitched echo. Other footsteps answer them from the depths, and music—thin, plaintive trills on a single string. Slowly his sight comes back. On a nearby wall Rashid recognizes graffiti and posters, and newspaper pages on the ground. News he doesn't understand, markers, warnings. Suddenly, while still trying to focus his eyes, he hears suppressed laughter behind him and feet quickly running past. Two bright white headscarves gleam above tightly-closed, high-necked smocks and long black pants. The two girls veer to the side and look back at him, standing close to one another, giggling. They know something, see something he doesn't. Rashid presses toward the wall. There are no nooks to hide in, just shuttered windows, stairs down to basements, and fire escapes. The two girls disappear in the dull light of a side street, mixing in with indistinguishable figures, shadows in the crowd. Only

their silhouettes—the headdresses, the long clothing—
hint at what side they're on. He knows he can trust them.
The whining string notes swell and intertwine with other
instruments: flutes, drums, voices. Rashid follows the
music. The walls of the buildings seem to encroach on
him, drawing ever nearer.

The alleyway is slowly filling up. People ooze in
everywhere. Dull yellow electric light spills out from dark
entryways. Soon he's surrounded by soft, warm bodies,
part of a moving wall of protection. Their moist faces
glisten; their skin and teeth and the whites of their eyes
glisten. Here and there a few have dark spots on their foreheads. Nobody pays him any attention. The crowd keeps
getting more tightly packed. A heavy but invisible cover
seems to lower over them. The air becomes still, echoes are
stifled. A low ceiling closes over Rashid's head, with cloth,
chains and lamps dangling from it. In a flash the city has
been transformed into an interior room. Corridors branch
off in all directions, an illuminated underground
labyrinth, buzzing, musty with the scent of incense and
coriander and infused with sweet smells—jasmine, mint,
vanilla, caramelized sugar. Stupefied, he pushes his way
through the colors—dull and bright—and past choirs of
haggling, sing-song voices. Bodies flow past clogged stands
festooned with goods, containers filled to the brim, baskets, shelves, wooden boxes, metal caldrons, stock jars,
sacks, crates, plastic tubs—it's a bounteous netherworld of
smoke, food and music, of knickknacks and intoxication.
He's entered the souk, the dark entrails of the city, its pulsing veins, its heart.

Carefully, ready to duck at any moment, Rashid
works his way through the throng. Everything green and
brown scares him. But they are other uniforms, he finds,
the outfits of clerics. No calls to prayer wind their way into

this false night, but still the chattering, dickering masses are full of holy figures with long beards and white turbans, prayer beads in their hands. He sees unveiled women bow their heads when one of the clerics appears in the crowd. Some of them go in twos, slowly, talking to each other, though they direct their gazes outward, distant gazes, the gazes of watchmen. None of them stand still or buy anything. It seems to Rashid as if they are all moving in the same direction. Whenever he comes to an intersection of corridors, he takes care to follow one of the white-bearded men. He thinks of the imam who saved him. At every turn the lights, colors and smells change, the spices, herbs, roots and dried plants. The catacombs are full of scarves and bolts of cloth that reek of moth balls, sandalwood and patchouli, shops selling sweets and coffee, gaudy displays of jewelry, eyeglasses, watches and electronics, leather stands giving off the scent of wax and tannic acid, stacks of carefully piled clothing, shirts, and ties, and neon-lit stands selling kitchen tools. A man with bare arms and a white apron scoops balls from a loaf and tosses them into a pot of boiling oil. Another turns chicken parts on a huge grill coated in charred drippings, beads of sweat on his chin. Rashid stands there staring, breathless. The sweating man calls out to him, Rashid shakes his head, and his eye lights on a white turban. Next to a garbage can full of paper plates and bones a cleric squats, begging. Bills flutter in the clay pot at his feet while he incessantly moves his lips with his head held high and his eyes closed.

Rashid freezes. He recognizes those fleshy lips. He knows those hollow cheeks and the big nose, the long, dark, frayed beard. Rashid takes a step back. The beggar opens his eyes. Black discs gleam in the middle of the reddened whites of his eyes. He has a heavy-lidded, steady gaze. He looks up at Rashid, straight at his face. It's as if a window has opened in the darkness. Light and cool rush in. Everything suddenly evaporates—his racing thoughts, the voices, the punches, pain, fear, shame. Light encircles the cleric's head, it's as bright as the light on the day when floods and heat and darkness will be banished. His illuminated head, cutting through the darkness, rises toward Rashid. His mouth is still silently moving, and now Rashid understands the Arabic words, the ancient dead phrases. You are on the right path, says the holy man. You're not a reprobate or blasphemous. You are righteous and humble. You are our man. You know us and we know you. You are a martyr. Go ahead. This is the right way.

The beggar drops his head, a bill drops into the bowl at his knees. The vision is over. Rashid looks at his turban, looks around. The cooks are still there, and the hungry customers, gesturing and shouting, hands grabbing paper towels, passing bills, tossing out paper plates. And the throngs behind him are still there, too, women with bundles of cloth, plastic containers balanced on their heads, other women with sunglasses on top of their shrouded heads, bags and children in their arms, men. So many men, and so many with beards and turbans. The crowd begins to carry him along again, and he finds himself in the middle, moving forward. He only has to lift his feet. Heads, shoulders, clothing all around him, and he can hardly see the stalls to his right and left, or the shops or merchants. He can tell only from the smells what they are selling. He staggers through a soapy puff of perfume and scented oils, then he smells wool and linen, cool and dry—perhaps carpets or mattresses, pillows, plush cloth. Occasionally groups are lit up and he can look someone in the eye, faces like portraits, as if he's holding out in front of him the frame they're in. Some come close up and look at him. A fat man comes out of a side tunnel, head uncovered, a grayish black beard enshrouding his round jowls. The moment seems frozen in time, and the man stands out from the crowd; he nods at Rashid and is gone again. A cleric with a black turban and gray vestments turns around, stops in the middle of the stream of people, looks at Rashid through his thick-rimmed glasses, and smiles. A young man holds his pock-marked face toward him as if he were posing for a photograph, the face of a warrior. The man shows Rashid his eye, swollen shut, and the seeping blue along his smashed cheek bone. Over his tunic he wears a tattered yellow military jacket—a fighter; the war is not over and the enemy is all around. The bodies close up around him again and carry him along. From a side tunnel come more people, strengthening the flow. Rashid recognizes a tall Arab wearing a red and white checkered Palestinian scarf over a shiny brown leisure suit. But the break in the crowd closes up again and the man is lost in the forward motion of the masses, all moving in the same direction as Rashid. Yes, he is on the right path. He knows everyone and they all know him. He hadn't betrayed any of his fellow warriors. It's life and death. That's why he's here. He shares the same secret they do. They are all close-lipped, all on the way toward a common goal.

Rashid just has to walk along with them. He can't fall over—the crowd would hold him upright. There's only one direction. Nobody is going the other way. The corridor has widened. The light has gotten dimmer. The music is softer. Rashid is pushed toward the edge and recognizes the stone walls again. Now he smells wood, fresh wood and glue and sealant. Beside him is the opening to a store room, half basement, half living room, jammed with bureaus, cabinets, chests and chairs—lots of chairs—and sofas with broad wooden frames. Families walk around all the stuff, children crawl on the furniture. The dealer stands in the middle, directing teenaged boys who are moving the furniture around, rearranging it, taking things in and out. He gets just a glance before the theatrical subterranean world of the souk is gone and the curtains close behind him. The crowd is less packed, voices scurry into the open, and their freed echoes bounce around the open spaces of another alleyway. From far up above comes some daylight. Planks and chairs and tabletops from the furniture workshop are leaned at the foot of the wall. An employee stands in front of the stuff with his arms crossed in front of his chest. He lifts his arms and shoos the crowd past. The crowd spills out behind Rashid and he's pushed into something hard and bulky. Two men carry a door-sized frame past him. They hold it up high and tip it. Flashes of light fill the inside of the rectangle, swaying, then they spill over and pour back out. The edge of a roof appears in the frame, windows, the surface of a wall, then they set it down, leaning it against a wall and fighting their way back through the stream of people.

Rashid carefully approaches the mirror and looks at the beveled border. Behind him, deep in the reflection, he sees the monotonous crowd streaming past, the long robes, the veils, the wide pants, the uniforms of the clerics, the rubber sandals. Some of the people slow down, pause a moment, smile as they pass by him. Only he is missing. He stands in front of the door, peering and waving, look-ing for the man who must be him. The man who waves back in a dirty, oversized tunic is old. He looks at Rashid, but nothing in his searching, uneasy eyes makes it seem he recognizes him. His hand drops to his side. The swollen rings under his eyes, the vertical wrinkles between his brows, and his sunken cheeks, all framed by a black mane, hair sticking out, and a patchy beard—everything looks ill, stunted, evil. Rashid runs his hand over his head, and his sleeves fall in wrinkles to his elbow, revealing his arm—gaunt like his exposed ankles and his entire body. He shakes his head and looks at the ground, at the black pebbly pavement. He looks at his dusty gray toes, the sinewy tops of his feet. He must keep looking. He must figure out who he was. He doesn't want to be this man, this hungry, unfamiliar man. He wants to see his own image. If he can find it, all he has to do is lift his head and he will see himself in the mirror. He knows he has to look for someone younger—not big, but strong and wiry; he has to look for a smooth face and a steady gaze. But there are just too many bodies, too many faces, fragmented, blending together, all there. They rush past, transforming into one another, but there's nobody he recognizes. Just once or twice a fleeting component that might have been able to help him, a gesture that disappears before he can put an identity to it. And always the feet, his feet—even they look unfamiliar, brittle street feet. They belong to him, he moves them, they move him, and he must flee: the enemy is everywhere. The camouflaged men are behind him, and they may be drawing near. He looks at the mirror again and sees only people like him—Arabs, a few Persians maybe, or Afghanis or Pakistanis or Indians. And there in the middle he stands, a grizzled young man with nothing left to do but wither and die. Or perhaps revolt. Not to be hunted anymore, not to sink anymore, dirty and mute. Rashid looks at himself. His shoulders are quivering now. He presses his lips together. He sobs. It's enough—Rashid doesn't want to see himself anymore, never again. He turns away from the mirror, following his dream, walking on. He walks with the others, jostling and shoving, forward. He needn't flee any longer. He's someone else. He wants to move on.

He begins to run. And he notices he's getting

stronger. The stomping and shaking gets his lungs going, which wakes his limbs. Everything gets brighter, clothing and faces. And a new smell fills his senses—no longer incense or grime, but rather a burning smell. It's fresh, bitter, alive. It attracts him, pulls him like a light at the end of a tunnel, like the sunlight at the end of the alleyway he's in. The people around him have gotten louder, more unruly. As if infected with Rashid's uneasiness, they walk faster toward the opening where the light is ever more glaring and dense. The colorful headscarves and black and white turbans transform into a festive pattern, giving the scene the look of a street fair. Between all the bouncing bodies streams a warmth, some sort of sense of anticipation binding all the movement. It's an outlook Rashid doesn't have. He only sees the wall of light. He looks at it like a scene from a movie, a mere onlooker. He wishes he could just run with them onwards—he doesn't need a goal in view, or fulfillment. He just hopes to stumble upon the secret of the fervent celebrations, the party, the fight. Up ahead the throngs of people are lit up and the pattern formed of headgear breaks down as the people scatter and run around shouting. He runs free and the burning scent fills his throat. He pauses. Light streams into the alleyway from all around. Now he can see out. Colors—a horizon of sand and green and red, and in front of it a searing flare. On the ground, framed by the end of the alley, a single figure in crazed motion. It twirls around its own axis, hardly touching the ground, rubber sandals on its feet and a tunic flying around its bare legs. The man holds with both hands a pole from which flames are shooting out like a dragon on a leash, belching smoke, uptight.

Others hustle out of the alley in front of him. Rashid steps into the light, into the open square filled with people surrounding the performer. He shrinks as the dancing dragon hisses and crackles, sparks raining down red and white. The long wooden flagpole is a glowing inferno at one end. The man begins to shout, drowning out the voices of the crowd, and his body pops up and down among the viewers. Now Rashid realizes he knows the man and recognizes his voice. In the ragged Arabic tones—"A" and "I," "A" and "I"—he hears his own name. It's Tarik, calling his name while spinning the burning pole. Rashid tries to make his way to the front of the crowd, but Tarik is moving away from him and the crowd is following. For a moment, Rashid can see Tarik's head between the heads in the crowd; he looks toward Rashid and laughs, jumps high and turns in midair, the burning pole making a glowing arc. The powerful move compels the viewers. Noise and applause and then they all start running, scattering. Rashid runs, too, following the fiery flag as it flutters into the distance, the flames consuming the last shreds of blue cloth. The fumes waft down and feet pound on the pavement.

Rashid laughs, his heart laughs; his heels spring, his joints flex and stretch. The ground flies backwards beneath his soles, warm and dry like the air. The smell of charcoal hangs in the air. The pavement becomes asphalt and the asphalt gravel. Shadows fly along with him, scurrying, surging, hopping, and others glide past as well, rigid and proud—the trunks of palm trees, columns, arches and domes. Rashid's shadow sticks near his feet, disappears at the top of his stride, then falls back to earth. Let out, finally let go, facing the spiraling sun, he makes up for all the untaken steps. He runs on, forward, forward, in concert with the flip-flops, the drumbeat of dirty feet, the singing of the masses, and meanwhile the oldest city in the world gets older. His steps take him to another open square with a scattering of buildings, trees and walls around it. Donkey carts and horse-drawn carriages roll over the bleached stone ground. Sheep and goats graze on a few patches of grass. Camels sway past casting long, hunchbacked shadows. It's Damascus, paradise. The ruins of temples loom above the walkers along with cedar branches and the gables of villas that would be at home high in the mountains. Believers live here, *They will be among Lote trees without thorns, among Talh trees with flower piled one a b ove another—in shade long—extended, by water flowing constantly, and fruit in abundance, whose season is not limited.* More and more arrive from all directions, men in tunics carrying holy books in their hands, squawking swarms of black shrouded women and excited groups of boys ducking in and out—kids on their way to a festival.

Rashid has lost sight of Tarik. Hundreds like Tarik are around. His flagpole has disappeared among a forest of sticks and poles holding up turquoise flags and images of clerics and white banners with black Arabic script on them. The smoke has blown away. But the flames have lit the horizon. Bright red flames burn atop the broad hills visible beyond the arches and spires of the old town. The barren clay-colored hillocks are sprinkled with bright spots—cubes and blocks in white and gray, shacks, barracks, multi-storey apartment buildings. In between a few mosques, their spires like watchtowers. The air between the low wastelands and the glowing heights shimmers and fluctuates. He feels the heat beating down on him and coming up from the ground. Rocky footing replaces the smooth ground. The walls are getting lower and the green patches fewer. The air has the odor of squalor, and smells of rotting and sewage. First there are shacks made of wood, wire and corrugated iron along the shining red path. Gravel crunches under the rubber sandals of the people in front of him and pieces of stone roll around beneath their shadows. The voices have died down to a murmuring chorus, and suddenly they stop altogether. Thin but penetrating comes the sound of loud-speakers, *Allahu akbar*, drifting down from the hills, out from the city flats, intertwining and bolstering each other above the pilgrims' heads. One after the next stops and turns to face the opposite direction of the sunset.

Rashid surveys the figures in front of him, the lamentations in his ears: "I" and "A," "I" and "A," *a 'l-la ilaha illa -'llah*. Then he too turns towards the Mecca he knows, to the east. He looks back and sees the crowds in the light of the setting sun. It's an orange army. An army of prisoners. From the foot of the hills stretching all the way back into the city they stand there in their fiery uni-forms, brought to a halt listening to Allah's call: *hayyi 'ala 's-salah!* Orange silhouettes. Oranges with shaved heads, oranges with prayer caps on, young and old. Oranges in signal orange outfits, oranges in the fields, in the marshes, all on the right path. They bow, emaciated and sullen, *hayyi 'ala 'l-falah*. So many oranges like him. They could do a lot together. They've broken out. They're headed out to pray, to fight, at sunset. *Go ye forth whether equipped lightly or heavily, and strive and struggle, with your goods and your persons, in the Cause of Allah*. The sky glows.

La ilaha illa -'llah. The calls of prayer die down, answered by the last reverberations of their own echoes. The army sets in motion, heading off to the west. *When ye travel through the earth, there is no blame on you if ye shorten your prayers*. A red wave washes uphill, carrying Rashid with it and sweeping those in front of him along as well, tinting the tunics and turbans, the banners and faces. Red lights up the dust and gravel, the unkempt houses with no windows or doors. The laundry hanging from ledges lights up red, red frocks, red sheets, red towels. The tent-like tarps stretched along poles around the shacks to protect them from wind and sun are red. Row after row they line the unmarked paths. Along the sides are garbage and grass, plastic, rusty scrap metal and piles of rotting fruit peels buzzing with flies. Those who live here have no time and no real home. Every nook captures shadows. They fall across the ground, cling to the walls. Rashid knows them well, the dogged, invisible movement like vines, they envelope the prison cages, too. Only now does he recognize the prison. It's rundown, forgotten, derelict after years of exposure and heat. But no one has escaped. The prisoners are still living in the stalls, without fences, doors or chains, without surveillance but still closely watched. Refugees forever. Only the guards have become invisible. A city of exiles and Rashid right in the middle of it. At the same time he sees the whole scene from a distance, from above, his likenesses behind beams and wire grids, the network of paths, the haggard masses, the pilgrims, warriors and clerics. He sees how the inmates all creep out of the holes in their tattered orange outfits. They cry, they shout with anger and joy. They walk along the ramparts, they form lines. The cages empty and the paths teem. The throng makes its way up the hills and reaches a knoll. In the bleak open space they stop. They stand side by side and listen, acidic sweat billowing from the orange outfits, a huge congregation under the open sky. Above the melee Rashid can see the roof of a mosque. Its minaret protrudes into the deep red evening like a budding plant stalk.

Prayers are over. But from the loudspeakers comes a familiar voice. Sometimes it sounds soft, other times harsh. The imam speaks—the imam from Damascus. He's talking to the believers, the prisoners—they are one and the same. The imam knows them all. He refers to each by name. Rashid Bakhrani, he says. You know the last suras. Rashid wants to answer, yes: *Verily the Day of Sorting Out is a thing appointed.* He understands Allah's language. But he cannot speak. The imam asks him, Is Allah not the wisest and most righteous judge? Rashid nods. He's a believer; he has followed the right path. He knows, *None shall speak except any who is permitted by Allah Most Gracious, and he will say what is right.* He knows how he must answer. Yes, I am Rashid Bakhrani. My father is Muslim and I am Muslim. I am a warrior. I don't want to open a shop. I've come from Hamburg to Damascus to fight. I know the Koran. *Those who believe, and fight for the Faith, in the cause of Allah, as well as those who give them asylum and aid—these are all in very truth the Believers: For them is the forgiveness of sins and a provision most generous. And those who accept Faith subsequently, and fight for the Faith in your company—they are of you.* He stares silently at the mosque's spire. The red has faded. It's gotten dark. The men wait, their shadowy faces turned to him. The whites of their eyes glow. They are his brothers. But still they are suspicious. They want proof, but he doesn't know the right word. The imam is silent. *Home,* Rashid thinks and hangs his head. That's not the right word, he knows. That word belongs to the doughy white face beneath the flood lights, the doctor. Only now does he notice the Islam-MP, Muhammad, the Muslim *chaplain.* He's here. He's expecting him. Rashid looks up again. Of course he's here. The dark face with sunken cheeks. Muhammad is standing next to him. Islam has finally arrived. He nods to Rashid, *be calm,* he says, *be patient.* You can see you have made it. Just look around. You have arrived.

Rashid turns around and sees he's at the edge of the knoll, not far from a steep slope. Beneath him as if in a deep crater is the huge city shrouded in night. It's ablaze as if the sun has fallen into the crater. Fire arches in clouds over the gorge, a reddish fog inside which bright blasts shudder and trails of colored lights flash. Now he also hears muffled, pulsing booms drifting up, the dull thud of explosions, again and again, as regular as a violent heartbeat. He gets it: the war is down there. He feels its tug. At that moment the crowd of people around him begins to move. They press to the edge of the slope and take him with them. He lets himself drop and tumbles downhill. He barely moves his feet. It's more like sliding down than walking. The bodies around him prod him on, catch him, push him onward again. Beneath him a warm, wheezing mouth opens up, getting hotter and louder. He plummets into it with the herd, hits bottom, and runs onward, past building fronts, street lamps and neon signs. He stumbles, rights himself, and lets himself be driven by the noise crashing over his head, whistling, buzzing and screaming sirens. His heart races; everything races. The entire street is a roaring wave, cars with open windows and tops, buses with bundles of people hanging out the doors, people walking beneath a forest of placards and scarves. Their heads jerk back and forth, dark faces mottled with splotches of the city lights. Through the red fog in the sky Rashid recognizes the huge watchtowers, outlines of the minarets—the parapets beneath the bulbs and spires. He's no longer scared. He drifts right down the middle of the rushing current of the street, accepted, indistinguishable from the others. The crowd has once again enclosed him amid warm, sweaty bodies—damp cloth rubbing against his skin, hands, shoulders, ankles—and shouts and whoops, which he breathes in. Jostling from all sides and laughter, rollicking and fierce. The stream begins to thicken and slow down, and the crowd starts to sway. Rashid grabs onto the man in front of him. Someone beside him braces himself by holding Rashid's waist. Someone's chest bumps his back, and hot air is exhaled on the back of his neck. But he's not afraid. Gazes fall on him and then look away again, all benign, all indifferent.

He lifts himself up on his toes and tries to see out over the heads in front of him. The street has opened up at a wide intersection. Turquoise flags stream in from all four sides, white scarves, placards decorated with images of the heads of clerics, vehicles with men sitting on top waving. Everyone thrusting toward the center of the crowd, packed in, lurching in this logjam that's absorbing all these bodies. Then there's a push back, and panicked shouts. The pressure makes it difficult for Rashid to breathe and he fights against it. He can feel the crush easing in front of him, up where the scarves have begun to flutter in the air, up and down, the corresponding bodies jumping up and down beneath them. The ground begins to shake. Rashid sees heads rocketing up and plunging down, rocketing up and plunging down, and the rhythm becomes uniform and creates a stomping pulse in his ears and limbs. Finally he manages to carve out some space as all the motion loosens things up. He jumps high and feels the air under his tunic, a ripple on his skin, a buffeting wind. Again and again he launches himself off the ground, and with every jump he lets out a low surge of breath; up high there are screeches all around. "A" and "I," up and down. The air is filled with fluttering colors, a festival. The crowd stomps, Rashid dances with his arms held high. He sees his arms are part of an undulating field of flapping, up-stretched arms. He wants to fly. They are all flying. They follow their hands into the colorful sky, shouting "I," "A." Hands are balled into fists and their voices bundle together as well, rising over their heads like a giant bouquet of balloons tied together by their strings.

Rashid pants. Burning smells hang in the air. His voice still fails, stuck in his throat, jerking and scraping with every hop. He searches for the word—he wants to go home, *home*. He is free, after all, and he wants to fly, to sing: *fly like an eagle 'til you're free*. He wants to go up in the Ferris wheel, into the sky, to look down on the big city, the fair, the undulating, dancing ocean, hands, flags, balloons. But the hands have become fists and the people are stomping and shouting in rhythm, "I" and "A." They are heading to battle. It's war. It's burning. The smoke cuts into his sinuses. The stomping and shouting gets louder, angrier. A reddish glow flickers on the faces, flames in the sky. Rashid sees a blazing form floating upright above the rows of people in front of him. It sways, stiff, puppet-like, its clumsy, charred arms leaving a black trail of smoke. Rashid's eyes water. The shouts swell. The black cloth crackles as it burns, and sparks shower down on the uplifted heads. The flames begin to die, and now it's dark. The bodies huddle together, the whites of eyes and teeth flashing around him. Feet continue to stomp. Rashid sees open mouths, upraised fists; embers rain down and singe his bare arms. Shouts, voices, the word, "I" and "A." He opens his mouth, scans the crowd, flakes of ash float down onto his face, onto his tongue. The ash is bitter and his tongue squishes it onto his gums. It sticks, then dissolves. His voice begins to come back. He shouts. They all shout as one, a single voice. They shout: *Jihad! Jihad! Jihad!*

VI. *Happy Ending.* No End.

They had already brought Abdullah back to the neighboring cell before midday prayers. Since then he'd been sitting on his cot with his back to the metal wall, gasping. Once in a while his hunched dull orange form twitches. His head rests on his knees covered by his arms. He's probably ashamed and crying, and the gasps are disguised sobs. Rashid has to keep looking up from his dictionary. Each time a black spot dances in his eyes. Abdullah is interrupting him. They've treated his foot. The white bandage glimmers through the dense fencing.

      This means, of course, his incessant pushups have finally stopped. Rashid had had a hard time getting used to the gasps that went with the pushups—really more of a panting. Abdullah had hurt himself while doing them this morning. No wonder. Three days earlier they had lowered the cots in all the cells so prisoners couldn't crawl under them anymore. Instead of being mounted thigh high, just below the ledge of the window grate, they now hover just off the floor. But now that you can't use the space beneath them, they take up half the cell. For three days Abdullah still managed to exercise despite the fact that there's no longer enough space. Before he had lain diagonally with his feet under the bed. Now he had to stretch out alongside the bed. He couldn't have his head at the window end because either he'd bump the metal sink in the corner or, if he shimmied into the middle, his face would be right

over the hole in the floor that functioned as the toilet—
and that reeked day and night. So he did his workout the
other way around, with his head facing the door and his
feet at the other end, one foot between the bed and the hole
in the floor and the other between the hole and the sink.
He would groan up and down until he was completely
exhausted. But this morning, at some stage he suddenly
dropped to his stomach screaming and cursing in Arabic.
He sat up, holding his bleeding foot—it had probably
slipped into the hole in the floor and caught on one of the
rough edges of the metal foot rests on either side. An MP
was instantly out front of his cell door. Here, on the corridor, they patrol alone. Hardly half a minute passes when
one of their outlines isn't seen passing by the bars of the
door with its two steel plates—one at ankle height and
another waist high—that could be opened to put on
chains. The MPs pace back and forth just like the prisoners in the *recreation area*. Their uninterrupted steps reverberate off the high point of the inverted-V roof which
peaks above the corridor running between the two rows of
cells.

They had all been worried about the long-
promised new housing. Then the move finally took
place—at night, under flood lights. When the sun came
back up it had been locked out. Whenever Rashid missed
his old cage, he tried to think of the blazing heat, the
swarms of mosquitoes, the stench coming out of the buckets, and the shame of being constantly on view. But his
mind always drifted off to the lost wilderness, the views he
had through the fencing, the playful shadows, and the colorful zoo he'd had around him—and he found himself
snapping back to reality feeling even more stifled, more
trapped, in his new metal box. Everything in the place—
the concrete floor, the roof and exterior walls made of

shipping container metal, the dense wire screens that form the walls between the cells, even the window bars and the metal cot and the door—was painted the same dull, industrial color, a cold greenish gray. Maybe that's why he had at first been reminded of the cooler—that and the fact that the new crate was smaller than the old cage. But actually the new building was hot and damp. Only when the MPs occasionally switched on the ventilation system did an unseen electric *fan* blow a little air through the bars of the door. Footsteps. Outside, the green tarps that keep him from being able to see through the razor wire are flapping in the wind. And next to Rashid, Abdullah's disguised sobs.

Rashid can't warm up to Abdullah. Jamal, on the other side, to his right, is a good neighbor. He can get the MPs to laugh. He makes jokes and sings. He likes Madonna and Britney Spears and Michael Jackson. Before this he'd been in a Taliban prison in Afghanistan where it had always been dark, always cold, and where they'd beaten him every day for seven months. Then the Americans freed him—only to bring him here. *They love me, that's why they wouldn't let me go*, he says. But now he's in the *interrogation room.* Beyond Jamal is a Russian, and beyond him a French Arab. It's impossible to get to know the prisoners on the other side because talking loudly isn't permitted. Rashid doesn't know anything about the prisoners to his left. Abdullah's too much of an obstacle. He's nuts—he doesn't talk but he's somehow still loud. He doesn't know any English. His letters he writes from right to left. They probably never get there; he's never received any responses in any event. You have to write your letters in English and make sure you don't write anything objectionable. Since they give you the paper and the felt-tip pen only for a half an hour, Rashid composes his letters in his head in advance. That's why he needs the dictionary. At first he'd used it to try to read a book on the American civil war. When that book was picked up, the older MP who brought books around asked him how the U.S. had civilized the world. Rashid thought for a moment and said: *They made war and they cancelled slavery.* The MP didn't seem too pleased with his answer, but when he delivered Rashid another book he brought him some *peanut butter* in a paper cup. He'd had to give the cup back.

He'd been given two unwrapped *twinkies.* Everyone knows what they are, but the word *twinkie* isn't in the dictionary. He'll have to write *cake*—that's the English word for a tort, a cookie bar, a baked good. What he really wants to write about is the shape, how funny looking they are—round and rectangular at the same time—how soft and crumbly the batter is, and how well the vanilla filling goes with it. *Vanilla cream.* After the first voluntary session of questioning he'd been given a Kit Kat bar, but they've figured out since that he likes *twinkies* better. He's kept one aside. He wants to eat it before it dries out, but he wants to wait as long as possible so he can just look at it—it makes him happy. As long as it's there he feels a little bit rich. It sits there on the metal sink like a little half-melted gold ingot, lined up next to the orderly row of things: soap, shampoo, prayer oil, prayer beads, toothpaste, toothbrush, and a plastic drinking cup—also a reward for a voluntary *interview. If you aren't willing to talk, you might never get out of here.* The metal sink gleams. Rashid polishes it several times a day with a dry washcloth. He can see himself in it. He feels an odd twitch whenever he looks at himself, like a tiny blot of electricity has shot from the sink to a point between his eyes. He sees the slightly blurry face of a prisoner, with dark hair and a beard like all the others, pale against the greenish gray background. The face looks as if it doesn't belong anywhere but here inside these metal boxes, the one he's actually in and the one in the reflection that he sees himself in. It's a tiny, orderly, closed world where everything fits together except for some small detail. An aberration, a mistake, an outlet. Something is slightly off. Rashid has to figure out what it is. He needs to find a reason he doesn't fit perfectly in this world. But in order to do that he has to understand what it is. He needs a plan to get him through this, and he'll manage to get through it only when he figures out the exit that is provided in this plan.

He makes sure everything is in its place, clean and manageable, the cell, the time. It's easier here than in the cage, where inside was actually still outside and everything outside came in from all sides. Inside and outside were always in flux even though it was just an iridescent little rectangle. Not everything that happened in that little rectangle was planned. The shadows played around with it, insects came and went as did lizards, buckets, excrement, the fenced-in forms of the other oranges, words, marks. The stalls were a no man's land the MPs couldn't control. Here in the cells there's only the monotonous prison norm. You have to adjust yourself to that standard—the smooth walls, the screens, the hole in the floor, the bed fixed in place, and the few flat surfaces: about two fingers-width at the base of the window frame, a hand's width around the sink, and an arm's worth at the end of the bed where the mattress doesn't quite reach the edge of the metal slab. Rashid keeps the black arrow and writing stenciled onto the foot of the green-painted steel bed frame meticulously clear: MAKKAH 12793 KM. Next to that he has his books. The olive drab flask. The towels, when they're dry—they dry quickly—and his clothing. An orange t-shirt has been added to the orange pants and top.

He takes his pants off at night. Anything he's not wearing he keeps neatly piled with the prayer cap on top. He folds up the light blue plastic blanket when he's not using it. That helps him bear in mind the endless cold of the four days he spent in a concrete cell after the time he hung his blanket on the door. There they'd taken away his blanket every morning and he quickly learned to be fond of his new, metal box and not to confuse it with a refrigerator. He always rolls up his prayer rug—a bath mat with reinforced edges—right after prayers and places it at the end of the cot. *I learned to pray and I do it five times a day.* The only thing he hasn't found a good spot for is the Koran. Jamal and Abdullah hang theirs from their window grates in face masks the MPs have given them to use as hanging baskets—the two of them consider the bed as unclean as the floor. The holy book in the white scale hanging on rubber straps makes a strange image through the screens, improvised, unsettling.

Every Friday we get sweets called cupcakes, or sometimes baklava, he'll write, and that the *twinkies* are something extra, just for him. There's plenty to say about the *twinkie*. It's the only thing out of place in his cell—that and his talisman. But that secret he'll keep to himself. It's up on the window ledge, a small red *Power Rangers* action figure. It looks like an invincible little orange. When the cage seems too small and time seems to stretch out in front of him forever he picks up the action figure. Others beat on the walls and shout; he just holds the statuette in his fist and waits it out. Sometimes it's hours before he opens his fist again. When he does he looks at the marks the plastic has pressed into his sweaty hands and he feels better. It's as if the *Ranger* has absorbed all the wasted energy wrung out of the cell. Whatever strength has been sapped from Rashid is soaked up by the *Ranger*. It's part of the prison, but at the same time it hints at another world, a world outside the prison—like the *twinkies*. An opening, perhaps. When he lies on his mattress and looks out the window, the outline of the figure is always in view at the base of the grates. Often he just looks at it and the background—the tarp-covered fences capped with coils of razor wire—fades into images of paradise. *Paradise*—that's where they all want to go. It's where the prisoners live together, eat together, sleep in one big room together, where they all wear white clothes and can come and go as they please. Security level four. A shower every day. Videogames. *And then perhaps release.*

The *Power Ranger* came with his dinner on the day after the first questioning session Rashid had requested. It was morning when they came for him. They didn't beat him. He wasn't blindfolded. It was a new room with bright recessed lighting, small, windowless, air conditioned. He was permitted to sit down. At his feet was a metal ring where they secured his leg irons. On the table in front of him was a tape recorder. They asked easy questions: whether he was religious, whether he sympathized with the 9/11 attackers, and whether he knew Al Qaida members. And they asked him again about Peshawar. He described everyone there despite the fact that he wasn't sure anymore which ones were real. Periodically they would tell him he would be freed, and then they would ask where they should take him. To Hamburg, he said. Then they would continue asking questions about the Taliban, the Muslim Brotherhood. He asked when he would be let go. One of them said: *We don't have any idea when you'll get to leave, we're just here to do our job.* That's when the thought first hit Rashid that it wasn't anybody's job to release prisoners—that there was no plan, not even a secret one.

If you don't talk, you might never get out, the young *chaplain* had said. You have to talk. This *chaplain* didn't have a name and he was strict, probably because he was always accompanied to the cells by an MP. Now Rashid had talked. But afterwards his cell seemed even smaller than before. He prowled back and forth like a caged tiger. It was as if he was starting over again from the beginning. Whenever he stood still, the metal ceiling and concrete floor seemed to clamp down on him and the walls to close in on him. The fear kept him from lying down. Things were basically the same as they had always been, but now a little bit worse. His breathing was fast, his heartbeat loud and irregular. He balled himself up on the mattress but jumped up again. He cowered beside the cot. He sat down in front of the sink and wrapped his arms and legs around it. He put first his hands then his feet into the toilet hole, as if he could dive or climb into it. He made sure not to touch the walls. He didn't want to make any loud noises. A double set of shadows fidgeted—one set cast by the lights on the hallway, the other by the floodlights outside the window. Morning came and daylight made the cell seem even more sealed off. Breakfast came and then lunch, and Rashid hit upon an idea that many others had hit upon: to cut open his veins with a broken shard of the plastic plate or with the *spork.* Imagining it made him feel better. But he handed back the utensil and began to pace again. Then they brought dinner. The steel plate at waist level was opened and the small black female MP shoved in one after the other a Kit Kat bar, a yellow paper carton with bright logos on it, and a big paper cup filled to the brim with Coca-Cola. *Enjoy,* she said.

He waited until the steel plate had been closed back up, then spread his dish towel out on the mattress. He put the food on it, sat down with his back to the door, and began to cry. He hadn't realized how good it would feel to be free. He cried real tears, warm flowing drops like the shower. He saw himself sitting at a table in the little McDonald's on the corner of Davidstrasse and Friedrich-strasse in Hamburg. As in all of his images of home, it was winter, and the hookers outside the window looked cold in their thermal tights and moonboots. Next to him Jenny excitedly ripped open her carton, tearing it. Jenny loved getting a *Happy Meal*—it was always a reason to celebrate for her, and she celebrated that way at least once a week. She would grab the greasy plastic bag holding the toy, rip it open, and then try to open Rashid's carton and grab his. But Rashid always held onto his and made her wait until she got impatient, shifting her weight from one foot to the other like the girls out front. She collected the toys on a shelf in her room. She didn't care whether the toys were doubles. But Rashid did—in fact he was more anxious about it than she was. She'd get to open his bag, but before he always took his time, carefully opening his carton. Suddenly he had a sinking feeling there might not be a toy in the carton at all. It turned out the only thing missing was the bag. Right in the middle of the fries was the little orange warrior standing there like a lost child. But it was-n't a toy—the figure was one of them, just like Rashid, a mirror image. It was dressed in the same outfit as him, with a mask decorated with flames and black eye patches and a silver belt where a *three-piece* could be attached. The feeling of reassurance and familiarity upon seeing the *Ranger* figure was so concentrated it hurt. It was as if Rashid had a visitor from back home. A visitor who wouldn't leave, a brother.

He pulled the packet of fries out of the box and underneath, unwrapped, was a cheeseburger. He began to eat. He felt better knowing the figure would still be left-over. Jamal's face was pressed to the screen; Abdullah watched Rashid from the other side. Rashid shoved a fry through the screen for Jamal, just the right size to fit through the mesh. Abdullah didn't want any. Jamal wanted more—the smell had permeated the air and wafted all down the corridor, and drawn the attention of the entire floor. After a while Rashid refused. He was happy when an MP showed up and shouted. Jamal gestured that he wanted a straw, but there was no straw. When they came to collect everything he had to chug down the remaining half of the Coke—he wasn't allowed to keep the cup. He wasn't allowed to keep the carton either. He had unfolded the carton and flattened it out, hoping to hang it up so he could look at the pink, blue, and white Disney cartoon on the sunny yellow top, and the four rounded yellow Ms on the red sides. Later he threw up but he savored the long-forgotten, unmistakable sensation of having been uncomfortably full. For the first time he dared to remember the kitchen table at home, Jenny's room, riding with Jenny in *Baba*'s delivery van, the weekend when his mother had gotten lost at the beach, the morning after dancing all night in a basement club, the square behind the old Jewish hospital, smoking a joint with Kemal on the city walls, the rollercoaster at the fair in front of the cathedral. Somewhere up ahead in the empty future, the *Happy Meal* had left a signpost and given his memories room to roam.

A rhythmic shudder runs through the cell. Abdullah is still sitting on the cot with his legs stretched out, but he's started to rock back and forth, his hands calmly sitting in his lap. He rocks silently, no longer gasping, and through the screen it looks like a film clip being looped over and over. Rashid flips through his dictionary. The book contains the entire world. A lot of things are outside, far removed, but the words still make their way into the prison. Sometimes they help him decide what to write. Sometimes he just scans the pages: *hole, holiday, holler, hollow, holocaust, holy, home, homicide, homo, homo - geneous.* He can't use all the words. They'll blot them out, just as they do in the letters he receives. He's already written twice about *Happy Meals.* The second time he'd written about Jamal getting one. In his was a miniature Barbie doll. It stayed on Jamal's mattress. He named it after his wife, Kathleen. She had yellow eyes, he said, and lived in Manchester, his hometown, *home.* They had captured him in Afghanistan. He's Muslim. He prays and sings. He talks to Kathleen and sleeps with her. He wants Kathleen to play with the orange *Power Ranger,* but Rashid always refuses. The *Ranger* is his talisman. Rashid doesn't talk to it, doesn't write about it, and hasn't given it a name. It's a talisman, after all, and brings luck—don't mess with it, or it won't work. Maybe it would even disappear. Like Rashid, the *Ranger* is only there by accident, out of place. He can see it there on the window ledge, but he keeps it secret. As long as it's there, something in the plan doesn't add up, something's off.

The letters start to blur. He closes the dictionary. A black spot dances in his eyes. *There's something wrong with my eyes,* he'll write. *It is more and more difficult to read, I think they are damaged.* A rhythmic metallic thumping echoes through the corridor. Somebody is banging on his bed frame. Someone else joins in. The MP has just walked past, and his footsteps are getting quieter as he gets more distant. The voices on the hall rise a little, hissing, whispering, murmuring. Abdullah rocks. Rashid gets up from the cot. Getting up hurts. Even though the abrasions on his ankles are healing, they've become swollen since he only gets to leave his cell to go to the shower and to his *interviews.* He adjusts the items on the sink, making sure they're perfectly orderly. He wipes away the crumbs beneath the *twinkie*. The tube of toothpaste is nearly empty. He'll squeeze out the rest and ask for a new one. He positions himself next to the window, his feet in the tiny space between the sink and the end of the cot, and rests his hands on the middle crossbar of the window grate. On the ledge below the orange skull of the *Ranger* glistens. Two wing-like shoulder pads, gold with white edges, extend out from its shoulders, shielding its arms and upper body. It's a good day. After midday prayers, the notebooks and pens will arrive. Rashid knows what he can write. Jamal is at a questioning session now and will have something to tell him. There's the *twinkie* that he'll eat at some stage today—at least half of it anyway. And for now Abdullah can't do anymore pushups.

Somewhere outside a metal bar squeaks, a car starts, dogs howl. But nothing is moving outside his window. If Rashid could make one wish—a prison wish—it would be to be able to lean out of the window so he could see what the building looked like from outside. He'd really like to see the place where he lived. When he squats down so he's looking out the window from the same level as the action figure, he can see the tops of the masts beyond the wall looming above the coiled razor wire atop it. The poles sprout heads—the flood lamps. In front of him is the green tarp-covered wall. He could reach it in seven or eight steps across the patchy, burnt grass. He could run his hands across the surface. He can almost feel the give of the waxy plastic. He can picture the dull shiny surface moving, the algae-colored tarp lightening and darkening to turquoise and black in the striations he creates as he drags his fingers across it. He feels the vibrations under the smooth skin, but not its source, wind and light. He presses his nose into the steel netting behind the tarp.

He spreads his nostrils and breathes deeply. His heart breathes, too, expanding and convulsing. He puts his cheek and ear to the surface. Since the time he'd been pitched out of the belly of the airplane, he hadn't seen the ocean again. But he could smell its proximity and hear it. The green tarp flaps in the wind, nervous and sluggish, as if it has given up hope of ever ripping itself free. It wants to blow away and open up the view of the ocean that spreads out beyond it. The ocean is there; it's always been there waiting. Its gentle rush creeping in through lulls in the camp noises, through holes in the fences. Its salt flavoring the air, rising unseen into the sky and seeping into cells, thoughts, and blood.

The footsteps in the corridor don't sound like a patrol. There are four sets, moving slowly, and a chain drags in unison with them. It's an escort, Jamal's escort. Rashid steps back from the window. Next door Abdullah sits up and presses his face to the sidewall. Rashid looks through the screen to his right into Jamal's cell. He stares at the front wall of Jamal's cell, where the door is. The footsteps near, and the orange outfit appears, wrinkled, shadows crisscrossing it. They open the door and the orange comes more clearly into view. They lock the door. Jamal hangs his head. A strange noise emanates from his throat, part breathing, part humming, a deep, absent-minded song. Now the steel plates are opened. One MP undoes the leg irons while another uncuffs him, undoes the belt and pulls the *three-piece* back through the opening. They close the plates and leave. Jamal remains standing at the door. Rashid sits down on his cot, pulls up his legs, and waits.

Jamal turns around, moving like a sleepwalker. The humming descends into his body and becomes a drone. He bends forward and puts out his hands as if he's blind. He squats. He slumps onto the cot with his back to Rashid. Rashid waits. Jamal turns slightly, scouring the bed for the Barbie doll. He takes it in his hand and starts to hum again. It gets louder, higher-pitched, up and down like a children's song. Now there are words. Jamal is clearly singing: *a young girl with eyes like the desert.* He lets himself fall back onto the mattress, holding Kathleen to his chest. *It all seems like yesterday, not far away.* Jamal is singing Madonna. Rashid leans forward and bangs his fist on the screen, once, twice. Jamal continues singing: *tropical the island breeze, all of nature wild and free.* Jamal, Rashid says. Jamal stops singing. He lifts his head, silent. *What happened,* Rashid asks loudly. Jamal clears his throat. *Shut up,* he says into Rashid's cell. *Stop your fucking prattle.* He rolls over, his back now to Rashid. Rashid leans back away from the wall. In the cell on the other side, water is splashing. Abdullah has stood up and he's leaning over his sink. Footsteps on the corridor. An MP nears, stops, then walks on. A shadow, the only shadow of the day, lies on the floor, a fine lace that runs from the base of the window into the toilet. The loudspeaker will crackle soon. Jamal grumbles. Rashid grabs a towel and stands up. He steps over to the sink, picks up the *twinkie* and carefully sets it down on the window ledge next to the red action figure. A few crumbs still cling to the edge of the sink. Jamal starts to sing again. *This is where I long to be,* he sings, *la isla bonita.* Rashid turns on the water and lifts his feet one after the other up to the sink. Abdullah unrolls his prayer rug. The loudspeaker crackles.

Dorothea Dieckmann

was born in 1957 in Freiburg, Germany. She studied literature and philosophy and now works as an essayist and literary critic. In 1990 she was awarded the Hamburg Prize for Literature. In 1996 she received the Marburg Prize for Literature for her novella *Die Schwere und die leichte Liebe* (*Heavy Love, Light Love*). In 1997 she was awarded the Stipend of the German Culture Foundation in Wiepersdorf Castle, and in 2004 she was a fellow in the Ledig House in Ghent, New York.

Tim Mohr

is a staff editor at *Playboy* magazine, where he has edited such writers as Hunter S. Thompson, John Dean, George McGovern, and Matt Taibbi. In addition to writing frequently for the magazine, he has also contributed to the *New York Times, Details* and *Time Out.* Prior to joining *Playboy*, Mohr spent six years working as a club DJ in Berlin. He graduated from Yale in 1992 and lives in Brooklyn.